Visions

Of

Darkness

A.D. Fletcher
The Jacob's Ladder
Series
Book 1

<u>Dedication</u>
This goes out to those few that helped me through this entire process. Without you, my vision would never have become a reality.

<u>Cover Art</u>
Karl Dahmer at Dahmer Art

My story begins....

Some say this is a tale of Astral projection. Some say it was psychic possession, others claim it's ramblings of an insane man pushed too far. Call it what you will, but it's my story.

It all started when I was six years old, for the most part I was a normal child. Well, as normal as one could be growing up in a hippy commune. Everything went downhill when I managed to fall from a tree and crack my head wide open. Seriously people, watch your kids.

With hippies as parents and them only wanting to rely on faith healing and the healing powers of nature, where could my care go wrong. I started seeing things, flashes of other realities if you will. The "doctors" as they called them said that the fall just opened a doorway to what others only dream about. They called me lucky, gifted, blessed and even the chosen. It's what I didn't tell them that was the real horror story.

During my waking hours things would only appear as a glimpse. It's like catching something out of the corner of your eye and it's not quite clear what you witnessed. While asleep things get more clear and bizarre.

We all dream, and some dreams seem so real that you swear they actually happened. For me it's living someone else's life for those few short hours. Feeling their pain, feeling their worries, feeling their death. It's never anyone having a great time, or a well adjusted existence. It seems to be the most brutal and tragic time for the worst possible person. The kicker is, however they were hurt or killed, I would wake up with a new scar in that location.

As you could imagine, this could mess up a six year old. Trying to explain where these scars came from to parents that were too fried to comprehend what I saw was always fun. Barb and Jim were good people but I'm not sure they were ready for parenting. Much less being the parents of someone as screwed up as me.

Barb and Jim, or Moonbeam and Star-dancer (as they liked to be called), thought it was some kind of a miracle. That was until the scars began to appear. By age ten, when the feds raided the commune for several major infractions and a few calls to the tips hotline, I became a ward of the state. The child services people believed that they were torturing me in some deviant rituals. They didn't believe that the scars and marks had nothing to do with them.

The next eight years were a blur of foster home after foster home, hospital after hospital. The constant tests and under-trained state head shrinkers became more of an annoyance than anything. They had either a person or a camera on me at all times while I slept. When that didn't prove helpful in how the scars showed up they tried strapping me down in 6 point restraints. Try getting a good night sleep with that shit holding you in place. They were convinced that it was my fault and I was causing them during night terrors. On my eighteenth birthday, I aged out of the system and was sent on my way. Kind of a "no harm, no foul" situation.

So I was out on my own with no job, no money and a hatred for the system. Nothing more than a scarred up kid on streets of Kansas City. My first step was to look for a place to lay my head. Everyone wants a place to call home and for a while I squatted here and there. I never really had that growing up so I took the first little rat's nest that I could afford. It was the type of place that didn't ask for references or credit checks. I felt lucky to kill two birds with one stone. The room I found was in an old apartment building that was in need of renovation. He told me I could stay there as long as I needed if I worked for him to fix the place up. The owner wanted to sell but nobody would buy this dump the way it was. So I worked slow to keep a roof over my head long enough to save money for a better place.

Some of the doctors I saw, while in the system, still wanted to see me from time to time to check on my status. They paid me under the table and a man's gotta eat, so I went. There aren't too many people lining up to hire a kid that made Frankenstein's monster look like a runway model.

Over the years the dreams got worse and the glimpses during the day became more clear. I learned that if I focus on them I can almost interact with certain ones. If I got bored or lonely, I would talk to them. They didn't answer me but it made me feel less anxious when they happened. Sometimes I would be out somewhere doing something and start up a conversation. It took me a few times doing this in public before I noticed that nobody else was actually there. People would stare and whisper about the crazy man talking to himself. I stopped doing this because I didn't want to be locked up again.

As I aged some scars would fade and some would become more vivid. There were scars on top of scars on top of scars. People didn't ask about them, even though they all wanted to know. Occasionally, I would get questioned by a small child asking out of innocent curiosity. But before I could say a word the parent would jerk them back next to them whispering loudly "don't talk to people like that" or "leave that man alone" and apologize for the kid being rude, but none of those parents would ever make eye contact.

It wasn't until I was in my late twenties that the glimpses and the dream world started to make sense. I didn't go out much or ever really want to be near crowds. I didn't live to far from the Westport area so I would hang out in the alleyway and listen to the music coming through the walls. I found that I had a love for the metal music. It seemed to speak of my pain and thoughts more than anything. One night, while listening to a few of the local bands I saw a flier for the annual psychic fair. I figured what the hell, if I can't get any answers it will at least be good for a few laughs.

I walk in and start scanning the area for a booth that doesn't look like it belongs at a cheap carnival. As I make my way through the room, I get that uneasy feeling of being followed. After years of looking this way and seeing what I've seen I should be use to it, but this time felt different. I walk a little faster trying to watch all around me when I come around a corner and run right into a 6'6" beast of a man.

"Where are you running off to?" the man says, looking agitated

"I'm not running, just taking in the sights. What's it to you anyway?" I fired off to this behemoth that was staring me down.

"Mother wants to see you." The man told me expecting compliance.

"Okay, but I don't know who mother is, nor do I care." I replied, as my annoyance with the situation grew.

"That wasn't a request. You will respect Mother's wishes and go one way or the other" the big man says, as he grabbed hold of my hoodie spinning me around forcing me to go where he wanted me to go.

"Well since you put it that way, let's go see this Mother." I say knowing I didn't have many options.

I could tell he sensed the sarcasm in my voice because the moment I turn, he smacked me in the back of the head and snatched me up by my hoodie. I felt I should try to lighten the mood a little so he didn't get any more reasons to manhandle me.

"So what do I call you, King Kong, Gigantor, what?" I asked, in the most smart ass tone I could muster.

"My name is of no concern to you." the man said sharply.

"Cool, but that's a bit of a mouthful so I'm going to call you 'No'. Hey No you can call me Scar." I say, hoping I could get some reaction from this man.

I knew I was starting to grow on him when his grip on my neck tightened as he shoved me through the crowd. We zigzagged down a few aisles and around a few booths for a couple minutes. Nobody seemed to notice, or they didn't care what was going on if they did. It's not every day that a behemoth is shoving a scarred freak around at arms length, but hey what do I know. Things looked bad for me when he pushed me out a stairwell door away from the view of onlookers.

"So No, where are we going?" I say, trying to stall. I didn't feel I should rush to a beat down.

"You will see shortly." the big man says, guiding me with his massive paw on my shoulder.

"Look, you're cute and all, in a rugged manimal kinda way but you're not really my type." I say, slowing my pace as I turn slightly to get a look at my escort.

"Less talk, more walk." the man says as he shoved me forward enough to throw me off balance.

Once I regained my footing I said "Strong silent type, I can see that. Fine lets just get this over with."

Just when I thought this journey was going on a bit too long, I feel his grip tighten and jerk me back and turn me to the left. I stand there for a second while he opened the door. No, as I have affectionately named him shoves me through the doorway. With two words I was consumed by dread.

"Wait here" the man says with enough authority to assure me there would be repercussions if I didn't do as I was told.

As the door closed I realized how pitch black the room was. No lights from beneath the door frame, nothing but darkness. I couldn't pick up any distinguishing sounds only a slight shuffling that I couldn't be sure which direction it was coming from. There was a thickness in the air of smoke from a struck match or candles being blown out, as if by some unexplained magic, flames shot from nowhere filling the room with a glow. I scanned the room allowing my eyes to adjust to the light only to notice an elderly woman sitting just a few feet away from me.

"Well hello, Scar is it? Or would you prefer your given name, Jacob?" the woman said in an almost gypsy-like voice

"Ummm, Scar is fine, nobody calls, me much less knows my real name. Who the hell are you lady?" I say doing my best to sound tough to the woman.

"They call me Mother. I've been expecting you for a while now." Mother said in a matter of fact tone, showing she knew more than she led on.

"Well, I don't know if I should be worried or feel special. So if you don't mind I think I will be on my way." I said making my way towards where I came in the room.

"You are welcome to leave when I am done with why I brought you here, but until then why don't you sit and make yourself comfortable. The more you fight it, the longer it will take." Mother said in a demanding tone.

"Well aren't you reassuring. I'm guessing nobody has given you an award for your bedside manner. I assume we are done with the getting to know you process, so let's do this." I say, letting the agitation come through in my voice.

"I wish it was that simple, but what needs done will not be as easy as you might think." Mother said softly in an attempt to calm me. It worked ever so slightly, but I was still a little leery of what's happening.

"If you say so. I just thought I was uniquely fucked up." I reply, taking a seat
"Not unique, but you are rare. Most individuals like you don't last but a few years before they can't handle it and break." Mother says as she places her hands on her knees.

"See, unique!" I say in a sarcastic manner to Mother. I wish this lady would get to the point. The longer I was there the more my mind started to drift.

"What we call your kind or better yet OUR kind, is Astral jumpers or hitchhikers. We can attach ourselves to…" Mother was saying when I butted in.

"Wait. Did you just say "our kind"? How can that be? I don't see any scars on you." I say letting my emotions get the better of me.

"If you would let me finish and not interrupt." Mother says sternly.

"Sorry, continue" I say apologetically.

"What I was saying, is that we can attach ourselves to others. Sometimes it's willingly on our parts and sometimes it's an automatic attachment drawn to someone's pain and distress." Mother says, taking her time to choose her words carefully.
"Mine only seems to happen while I'm sleeping, and usually it's shortly before their horrific demise." I say, while my body shakes with a chill running down my spine. The discussion of this has always left me with an uneasy feeling.

"As you learn to control the gift, you can see what has to be done to change the circumstances. Like you, I receive the scars but when the person's soul rests peacefully, the scars will fade and even disappear. If the situation is not rectified, the scars will consume you and be more prominent." Mother states, as she pushed up her sleeve to reveal a thick scar approximately five inches long.

"And you can help me with this?" I asked with my interest peaked.

"Only if you open yourself up and allow me and the spirits to guide you." Mother says as she spread her hands out to her sides.

"Spirits? What spirits?" I ask, feeling uncomfortable with where things seem to be heading.

"That feeling you get that someone is watching you, or the glimpses of something you can't explain. That's the spirits trying to reach out to you." Mother tries to explain.

"Oh Okay, I thought I was just nuts. I talk to them but they never really do anything." I state, sitting forward in my seat to lean on my elbows.

"Maybe you just aren't listening well enough. I've noticed you have an issue with that." Mother said raising an eyebrow at me, showing she can give sarcasm just as well as it's given.

"Hey! I resemble that remark." I say with a grin. Mother shot me a look of disappointment and contempt. Oh well, it's in my nature to be a smartass. Seeing this bothered her I say, "Sorry, I had to do it. I will try to be serious."

We talked for what seemed like days. It's hard to know what time it is when there's no windows and the only light we had was candles. No brought us food and beverages every now and then. I never grew tired or even had the urge to relieve myself. Topics were covered, breathing exercises were tried, meditation was attempted. Some things I'm going to work out for myself. She explained that these jumps or possessions were different for each of us but the results of the ending seemed to be the same. Scarred all to hell. The only way to get rid of these scars and stop them from piling up is to put the spirits to rest once and for all.

I saw Mother for a while after our original meeting. We met up once or twice a week for a year, then meetings became further and further apart as I became more in control. I was managing to have a small number of scars fade by doing what I had learned and kept some of the potential new scars from forming.

Through my ongoing training and practice, I learned that by focusing on a particular scar hard enough, I could take myself back to that memory. I tried this technique on the smaller ones but was still too afraid to go for the big, brutal, nasty scars at this time. I was told that to bring some of the situations back to the front of the list there's no nice way to say it, but to open the wound and have the pain deliver me. Waking up with them is one thing, I already felt the pain once. I'm not exactly in a rush to go through that again. Plus, have you ever tried to cut through a scar before? That shit is not pleasant. I've stopped going to the doctors altogether. They couldn't answer any questions and it was getting in the way of what was really going on. They wouldn't believe me if I told them how I was spending my time, and there would be a trip I didn't wish to go.

One of my more recent excursions to darker side of reality, the experience was a little too close for comfort. I was in the body of a girl that I've seen several times before. She delivered food for this little Italian restaurant. She always seemed nice on our interactions. By nice I mean not running in horror from the freak covered in scars that answered the door. I could see through her eyes, hear everything going on around her and sense her emotions. The training was beginning to pay off.

She was standing in what seemed was a public restroom fixing her hair. It was short, black and off of her shoulders. She was wearing a black shirt with lettering on it saying TTFA. I've heard of those guys. I've sat in the alley many times while they played. Then came a pounding on the door. I could feel the vibrations and her become irritated.

"Hold on, I'm almost done!" she shouted, full of annoyance

"Jenny, hurry up! You got deliveries stacking up." Came the voice, sounding authoritative

Her name was Jenny. Eight months of her bringing my food at odd hours and I never knew her name, nor did I ask.

"Fine, I'm going. I'm not staying late this time. There's a show tonight so these will be my last drop offs and I will bring you the receipts tomorrow when I come in for my check. Okay Sal?" Jenny said, demanding. I could tell this girl was a fighter with a it's my world and you're just living in it attitude.

"Whatever, just give me a heads up when they get delivered and at least try to get them the food while it's hot." Sal said, in the tone every boss gives you when you want something.

"Yeah, yeah I know what to do." Jenny said with a hint of annoyance.

"Enjoy your show." Sal said, as he checks over incoming orders showing he couldn't care less what Jenny did.

Jenny got a list of all the addresses and loaded the food into her car. As she began inputting the addresses into her GPS, I recognize some of them. A few hotels on the plaza, an apartment a few blocks from Westport and then one address that just jumps out to me. It's for an empty lot across the street from my place. I scream to her not to go, but she can't hear me. She hits the route setting and fires her 1984 Camaro up, letting the engine rev. Once it's warmed up Jenny hits play on the stereo and the metal begins to blast as she slams it into gear. Gunning the car and cutting the wheel she tears down the road continuously checking the time.

"Only forty-five minutes till the bands go on." She says, thinking out loud. Her frustration was showing, but she believes she is alone. Everyone acts different when they are alone.

I don't know how to let her know that she probably won't be making that show, or any others for that matter. There's gotta be someway I can make her realize that the last delivery can be her final one.

By no fault of her own something bad is going to happen to this poor girl. I'm not sure what bothers me more, the fact that I've met her and have never been inside someone I've actually talked to before, or that there's nothing I can do to stop what is about to happen. I watch intently as Jenny makes her deliveries. A drunk businessman at this hotel that paid too much, a man at this hotel that was clearly expecting someone else at the door. When the door opened and this scrawny man in a gimp suit sprung out then automatically hid behind the door apologizing when he saw the food bags, I felt her smirk.

"$32.50 for the calzones and don't forget to add one hell of a tip. I'm going to need it to drink away what I just saw." Jenny says, with her hand out stretched waiting for the money.

"I am so sorry for that. I was expecting company. I hope this covers it." The customer says taking the money out of his wallet and placing it in Jenny's hand.

"That will do, enjoy your night." Jenny said as she stashed the cash in her back pocket.

A hundred dollar bill not too bad for seeing professor spandex jump out I figure. Jenny is acting like she has no care in the world except getting to that show. She checks the time and notices that the show starts in eighteen minutes.

"One last delivery and it's on the way." Jenny mumbles to herself as she heads back to her car.

The address looks familiar but Jenny can't remember ever seeing a house there. She's delivered all over the city for years and knows these streets like she knows every lyric to her favorite song. I scream inside her head to just forget this one and go to the show. Jenny pauses for a moment like she hears me, but dismisses it and continues on the way.

"Where the fuck is this place? It's like I'm driving in circles. I'm going to be late, late, soooooo late."
Jenny grabs her phone out of the passenger seat and starts scrolling through the call list till she finds the name she was looking for, Sarah. She hits call and waits.

"Hey shithead, where the hell are you? You were supposed to pick me up 15 minutes ago." Sarah yelled over the music.

"I'm running late, boss has me dropping off food before he will pay me for the entire shift."

"Well hurry up, they started early!" Sarah said holding the phone out for a moment so Jenny could hear the band on stage.

"You went without me? What the hell?" Jenny says with a hint of anger in her voice.

"I wasn't going to sit around and miss this lineup. Jody picked me up on the way since Louis is playing. How many more stops you got to do?" Sarah asked sounding more distracted than concerned.

"Oh okay. I got one more stop and then I will be there, and I made decent tips so I can get some merch." Jenny said, checking the time again.

"Word, alright hurry the fuck up! Later." Sarah said, then hung up.

Jenny grabbed the delivery slip off of the bag and scanned it for a number and name of who placed the order. Boris Drago with the number and address was written sloppy on the bottom, partially smudged by grease. She reached for her phone once more and then as if out of nowhere she sees the address on a mailbox. The place looked run down and out of place. The house was an older Victorian with dark paint, windows covered with a layer of filth that can only come from years of neglect. The rest of the neighborhood was either apartment buildings from the 50's, one of which I lived in, or cookie-cutter pre-fab jobs. Those were all the same color and design with manicured lawns done by a service.

The street lights were burned out in front of the house while a single porch light lit the way. Jenny let her eyes take in the sight of the property. The side of the house was almost consumed by ivy and what looked like black roses. As she stepped around the remains of the small wooden gate she noticed a light moving through the windows as if it was a person was carrying a candle to see. Jenny made it up the stairs, careful not to fall through, and when she reached the huge red front door looked for a doorbell. After not finding one she grabs the brass knocker and slammed it against the door, hard, three times. On the third knock the porch light flickered and went out. Jenny reached into her pocket to grab her phone so she could use it for light and realizes she has forgotten it in her car.

Jenny noticed a light through the door window and heard the lock click. The door started to open slowly. "Hey dude, I don't mean to be a bitch, but we need to speed this up. I got some place I was supposed to be 20 minutes ago, so how about......." Jenny stopped mid sentence and looked at the massive form that stood in front of her. It must have been every bit of seven foot and took up the entire doorway. The candle light must have been playing tricks on Jenny and I, because what stood there didn't look human.

I scream in Jenny's head as loud as I could hoping she could hear me. I think it must have worked because Jenny tosses the bag of food in the direction of the monstrosity and saying "Keep it!". As she turns to run, her and I feel something sharp digging into her shoulder and yanks her body back into the darkness.

The grip on her shoulder was released as she continued to her rag doll flight. Her body limp and gliding, while Jenny's mind was frozen in terror. There is nothing more upsetting to me than watching the events unfold before my eyes and just be a passenger along for the ride. The void felt as if we were hovering through the pitch black air. Her eyes scanned the area searching for some hint of light. Jenny's body seemed to turn mid throw. Then without warning a hard crack to the spine and I felt her head come in contact.

I was jolted awake. The pain I felt in my back and head was real enough but I don't know how she died. I needed to check my body for new scars. Something to point me in the right direction. I yank off my shirt and run to the mirror. The only new ones found are what look like claw marks made from when she was grabbed and thrown, and they were bleeding. There's only one person I call that might know what this means.

"PUT MOTHER ON THE PHONE NOW!" I yell into the phone.

"Mother's busy, but she wants to see you." No says in an authoritative voice.

"I don't care if she's busy, put her on the phone!" I say, getting more agitated as the seconds pass.

There's a long pause on the other end of the phone. I could hear muffled voices that didn't sound happy.

"She says she will be at your place in an hour, so be ready." No said as matter-of-factly as possible, then hangs up the phone.

I pace the floors of my rundown rats nest that loosely resembled an apartment. Thoughts were bouncing uncontrollably in my mind. Nobody has ever been in my place. Even as much time as I've spent with mother, I didn't remember ever telling her where I lived. What do these bleeding marks mean? Why did I not see Jenny's death, only the attack? What or who was the thing that grabbed us?

Minutes passed like hours as I waited for Mother to arrive. When I figured it was taking too long there was a knock on the door.

"Who is it?" I bellow from the far end of the hallway.

"I told you I would be here in an hour, it's been an hour." Mother states, showing her impatience.

"Sorry, come in." I say as I unlock the door and start to open it.

"So what's the emergency that you had to demand a meeting?" Mother asks in a serious yet concerned voice.

I look down the hallway to see if there was anyone else with her. Once Mother was inside, I slam and lock the door. Turning towards her, I took off my shirt and tap her on the shoulder.
"This." I say in a shaky voice.
Mother turned to face me and is stunned by the sight. She steps forward to investigate the wounds. There were four large gashes that appeared to be made from a gigantic claw.

"Did you see his face?" she asks in a worrisome tone.

"Face? No. It happened so fast. All I know is there was a massive silhouette in the doorway of a house. That house!" Jacob stops mid word and took off running to the window.

"What are you doing?" Mother asks, now more confused than before.

"The house was right there, RIGHT FUCKING THERE!" I say, pointing to a vacant lot.

Mother spread the blinds with her fingers and leaned close to the window. She looks back and forth down the street. Not seeing where I was talking about, she tries to follow the direction that I was pointing with her eyes.

"In the empty lot, I thought you said it was a house?" Mother questions me as she squints her eyes to see better.

"I did, or it was. But it's not there anymore." My voice cracking under the pressure of feeling like I've completely lost my mind.

"How do you know it was there, right there in that spot?" asks Mother

"I saw the address and I saw my building as the woman looked around to see where she was going. Her name was Jenny, she delivered food for a living." I stutter on that last fact.

"Okay, well were there any more details you can remember, the weather, time of day, anything that could help?" Mother asks as she pulled out a notebook and pen ready to take notes.

"There was her car, it was an older model Camaro. She parked it on my side of the street. I don't see it out there now." I say as I peek out the window.

"It was night and the roads were wet like it had rained earlier in the day." I say, racking my brain.

"It hasn't rained in weeks. Well this could be an old one that just latched on to you and became attached to your gift." Mother claims.

"No, no, no, it can't be old. She just delivered food yesterday!" my tone starting to sound more upbeat.

I begin digging in my pocket for my phone when the thought hit me. Then I remember setting it on the chair near the hallway. I dart across the room and start scrolling through the apps until I find it. Once I read the screen I turn it towards mother.

"What do you see?" I ask.

"The weather forecast and there's nothing about rain till Friday." Mother says, wondering where this was going.

"It hasn't happened yet! I have three days to save her!" I announce, with a new vigor in my voice.

Mother and I discuss more details and try to formulate some kind of a plan while she bandages my wounds. The blood seemed to soak through the bandages. Ideas flowed but nothing of real worth. My thoughts of ordering food for the two of us just to get a look at her didn't go over well at first, but once I say I would pay, Mother agrees it was a good plan. As I get ready to call, Mother stops me.

"Hold on, let's see what Sebastian wants and you can buy his also." Mother says, as she washes her hands.

"Who the hell is Sebastian, and where is he?" I ask, feeling like I'm missing something.

"I believe you call him 'No'. He's in the car waiting patiently." Mother says with a smile.

"Ha ha Sebastian, that's funny but I prefer No." I say with a chuckle.

Mother got out her phone and within two minutes there was a knock on the door, it was Sebastian. Mother signaled me towards the door to let him in, the entire time giving me a look like she knew what was going to happen.

"Sebastian, come on in." I say holding back the laughter.

"I'll make you eat that grin." Sebastian says, full of attitude.

"No thanks, but we were going to order Italian if you want any." I say to him.

We walk down the hallway to join Mother. I hand out delivery menus from the drawer of the night table. It takes a few minutes for everyone to decide what they wanted. I call in the order, and then we just wait to see if we get lucky enough that Jenny would be the delivery driver.

The three of us wait, two more anxious than the third. Sebastian stood like a statue watching out the window. He was always vigilant when it came to mothers protection. I'm not sure what happened to bring them together, or if there was a relation that I was unaware of, but nobody got close to mother without dealing with him first. I know he could snap me into pieces if he wanted, but mother seems to like me and won't allow it. I give him shit, but I know he's just doing his part in this twisted play we call life.

Just about forty-five minutes pass when I hear the roar of an engine ripping down the street. The sound echoes off of the buildings. Something older and not one of these Eco-friendly pieces of euro crap. I go to check out the window, but Sebastian is blocking the entire window frame except for an inch on his left. I sneak a peek when I hear tires squeal to a halt.

"Foods here Mother" Sebastian states in his normal, angry sounding tone.

"Nobody move, I'll get the door, and pay for it all. And carry it all and deal with everything." I say sarcastically. Neither Mother nor Sebastian budge in the least or offer assistance. When the knock comes from the door.

"Sergio's Italian, I got your food." Comes belting through the door.
"Coming!" I yell to answer.

"It's her, it's Jenny!" I say as my pitch goes up when I say her name aloud. Getting nervous as I approached the door. I thought I might frighten her with my appearance since she's never seen me in the light before.

"Sorry it took me so long to get to the door." I say nervously.

"It's cool, slow day so I'm in no rush." Jenny says, pulling the receipt from her pocket.

"So what's the damage?" I ask Jenny, getting my wallet out of my pocket.

"$37.89, a little more than your usual order." Jenny says looking at the receipt.

"Oh yeah, I got company over." I say as I dig through my wallet.

"Wow company, here I thought you were some kind of hermit. I mean I've only ever brought over single serving items." Jenny says, as she is now the one getting nervous.

"I don't get out much so no harm no foul. I tend to avoid crowds and individuals with the way I look and all." I say, pointing to my face.
"What's wrong with how you look? I mean, so what if you got your ass kicked by Edward Scissorhands. At least you lived to tell the tale." Jenny says, smiling awkwardly.

"Well maybe, I will try to get out more. I like metal, do you know of any shows coming up?" I say trying to be smooth. I can feel Mother's eyes burning into the back of my head.

"The only reason I say metal is I noticed your shirt." I say, trying not to act like a crazed stalker.

"Oh, yeah there's a show Friday down in Westport." Jenny says

"Thanks, maybe I will stop being a hermit for a night. Oh, here's this before I forget." I say handing her some cash.

" I don't have change for a fifty." Jenny says

"Keep it, consider it a tip for the food and conversation." I say, taking the food.

"See you around, hopefully Friday." Jenny said with hopefulness in her voice.

"You can count on it." I say awkwardly.
"Doors are at nine, shows at ten. Don't be late." With that being said she was down the stairs and out the door.

I walked back to Mother and Sebastian to pass out the food, trying to act like I don't notice the dirty look. The glare from Mother didn't phase me, because for the first time someone didn't look at me like a monster. And that person was a woman.

Ideas were bounced back and forth. Sebastian had a few ideas but they mainly consisted of me kidnapping Jenny, or calling it a loss and move on. We tried to explain to him that neither one of those were viable options. We finally settled on a plan and it had to work. Only a few days to get the kinks out.

Sebastian kept watch on the vacant lot across the street for any changes. I asked him several times if he wanted a break to rest but he always refused. So I took advantage of the time and went to get a few provisions that were going to be necessary to pull this off. Everything I get I charge to the apartments as equipment needed for repairs and renovations. Going off of the list Mother made up, it seems like either she's done this before or it's just guess work. Some of the things made sense, like walkie-talkies and bandages, but I'm not sure why I need 200 pounds of rock salt.

Time moved slower and slower and all but stood still. Friday morning came and we knew the moment was closing in. Sebastian still eagle eyeing the street and vacant lot for even the slightest of changes. He noticed an older van drive by on occasion but never thought much of it. As the sun started to set the van pulled up in front of the lot and parked. By some strange connection Mother began to convulse and pointed at my shoulder. My wound began to bleed profusely, soaking my shirt and running down my pant leg. I dropped to my knees and Sebastian turns to catch me and stopped me before my head cracked the edge of the countertop.

As suddenly as it started, it was over. Sebastian set me in a chair and went back to overseer duty. His gaze was met by a mammoth house in the once empty lot. Mother and I snapped back to clarity when those two words were spoken.

"It's here." Sebastian announced as plainly as you would say the mail has arrived.

Sebastian took a few steps back from the window and Mother and I moved in to see. It was the house. There was nothing blocking the sun yet the house appeared to be in a constant shadow covering all sides. An obsidian nightmare that had a shimmering haze hiding details. I'm awestruck and horrified at the same time. Mother explains that it must not be fully formed, or has a protective barrier to keep the unwanted prying eyes at bay.

The sun started to set around 5:15pm. The dimming sky provided the perfect cover to put our plan into action. I begin spreading the salt around the property line. This will prevent anything supernatural from entering, as well as leaving. Trapping it inside may not prevent Jenny's attacker from trying to get her, but it will stop it from getting away or getting any outside help. Everyone one knows that a cornered animal is more dangerous. It also makes them unpredictable.

Once the salt is laid out leaving no gaps to weasel through, I bury five foul smelling pouches in certain areas that mother picked out. I head back up to my apartment to get cleaned up. No sooner do I get changed, the rain starts. It seems to only be raining around the house. Mother points to the street and nods for me to see. I notice all the salt being washed away. The rain stops and the haze vanishes from the house making it more clear. The pitch black house looked every bit of a hundred years old. The once obsidian outer shell is now a dark flat black reassembling soot. The lattice panel was covered in vines of black flowers that are constantly in motion. The filth covered windows seem to shift just enough to change one's perception of the structure. It appeared to be two stories high with a window that could be an attic. A singular light moved from window to window in a fluid motion as if there were no rooms or restrictions. So our plans had to change.

Mother was going to be the one now to try to hitchhike Jenny. She has more control than I do and believes she can offer influence into her decisions. Sebastian will help me gain access to the house but has to be back to protect Mother in her vulnerable state. I start to head to the house and get stopped by Sebastian's massive paw.

"What's up big man? I got shit to do." I say, checking over my gear.

"Take this, you're going to need all the help you can get." Sebastian says, handing me a bag.

"Awe, you remembered my birthday! Lets see what you got me." I say, feeling the heft of the bag.

I knelt down and opened the bag to find a jacket made from what looks like a type of leather. It's thick, but pliable. So, I tried it on. Once buttoned, it seemed to tighten and form to my body like a second skin. I throw my black hoodie back on so I don't look so out of place. Nothing screams weirdo like a skin tight leather shirt. I nod at Sebastian as a thank you and head out the door.

Once I'm standing in the presence of this living dwelling the fear sets in. not fear for my safety, but fear of failure to stop what I saw. I never had much faith in anything, but I could tell there was something greater and more powerful than anything I've ever heard of at work. I searched the exterior of the house trying to find a weak link to gain access, but was coming up empty. That's when I noticed a pattern emerging in its rearranging. There was a brief hesitation and blurring of the basement window to the left of the front porch. The blur only happened when the light wasn't on it. This is where I needed to go through. This is where I would test my metal.

I back up a few paces and wait for my chance. The light begins to flicker and I can see the blur. I take a running start and drive at the window. I shield my eyes from broken glass in anticipation of the impact, but feel nothing until I hit the floor with a thud. Opening my eyes to a squint to look around, giving my eyes a chance to focus in the pale glow of my flash light.

At first the only objects I can make out are a few stone columns and the dirt covered stone floor. I spin to find the window that I entered from and find a solid stone wall. The vaulted ceiling and stone walls look too ancient to belong in a house that just popped out of nowhere. I follow the carving on the wall till I find a spiral staircase in the middle of the room. Each step made of bone and mortar seems to hoover on its own.

I see a flicker of light that could only be a flame bouncing against the stairwell walls above me. I check the time and pull out my radio to let Mother and Sebastian know that I made it inside. Once I turn it on, I hear white noise with a low murmur pulsating through the speaker. The radio being no use in here, my only hope is that Sebastian saw me make it in so they can start their end of the plan.

As I make my way up the stairwell slowly, I turn my flashlight off so I don't draw any unwanted attention. I stop moving when I reach a solid wood door at the top of the stairs. I can hear a voice just beyond the door. It has a heavy accent that sounds vaguely like what I've heard before at a Russian grocer I frequently visited years before.

"He's placing the order." I thought quietly to myself.

Knowing the order has been placed, I know that I have about 45 minutes to end this and hope mother can convince Jenny to keep going and skip this delivery. I hear the heavy footsteps move away from the door and sound like they are heading up more stairs.

Once the thumping of the steps seemed far enough away from the door, I figured this was my window of opportunity to enter the main floor and get a lay of the land. I attempt to open the heavy door and realize I have to put my weight behind it to get it to budge. Leaning into the door I open it enough to get a glimpse. I pull a mirror out of my cargo pocket and use it to see behind the door so I wouldn't risk sticking my head out and getting it taken off. Not seeing anyone or anything I have no choice but to make my move.

I get the door open wide enough to slip through while keeping low to the ground. I quietly get through and begin closing the door when I feel the footsteps. They still feel faint so I know I have to hurry, but they are heading my direction. I get the door closed and move to the right, away from the incoming foot steps. The vibrations are preceded by what I guess is the light of a single candle. I make my way to what I can only imagine is furniture covered by drop cloths and duck behind in the pitch black shadow.

I shift slightly to try and see what is holding the candle. The air in the house is thick with a dampness and an odor of decaying compost or rot. Leaning into the drop cloth covered object, I notice there was something oozing through the fabric. I shudder at the thought of what it could, be but don't let it deter me from what I came here to do. That's to save Jenny.

It took me a moment for my vision to come into focus with the dancing light of the candle. The figure cast a silhouette, and I couldn't make out any definite shapes. The parts that were illuminated by the flame, were cloaked by a tattered robe of some sort. The base of the candlestick was hidden by the robe as well. The cloaked beast released the candle from its grasp and whispered something barely audible causing the light to float on its on back up the stairs. As I watched it float away, I hear the rumble of an engine and the slam of a car door coming from outside. A moment later I hear three pounds of the door knocker on the door. Then, it spoke.

"Your friends let you down." Said a voice from the darkness. Then the front door began to open.

"Hey dude, I don't mean to be a bitch, but we need to speed this up. I got some place I was supposed to be 20 minutes ago, so how about......." Jenny stopped mid sentence.

There is no reason to hide any longer since it knew I was here. I jumped up and darted toward the doorway to try to stop it from grabbing her. I snatched a chair on my way by, and was hit hard in the chest like the force of a freight train. It sent me flying backwards with the wind knocked out of me.

As I hit the wall, I saw Jenny's limp body hurled at the stairs. I lay there unable to move and hear the thud of her back hit and the cracking of the wood as her head made contact. The feelings of helplessness and failure start to consume me and I know I have to do something, anything. I'm not going to let this thing hurt her or anyone else again.

I stagger to my feet, the pain breathing a fire of life into me. If I can stand, I can fight. Taking a few laboring steps, letting the cobwebs shake free. I need to do something to draw its attention away from Jenny and give her a chance to come to and get somewhere safe. I notice the creature raising its arms and muttering a language that I can't understand. The front door and windows began to fade being replaced with solid walls. It's sealing us in. With the exits gone, more candles ignite and burn bright.

"Hey you!" I yell, getting the creatures attention.

The beasts cloaked head turns slightly in my direction.

"Yeah you, tall cloaked and nasty. Did you forget about me?" I say spitting a mouthful of blood onto the floor in the things direction. I can tell my technique is having some effect on it. I'm not sure if drawing it to attack me was the best plan, but if it gives Jenny the time to get her wits than oh well. I just hope this armor that Sebastian gave me works.

"Come on princess, let see what you got." I say, as I regain my bearings.

"If you're trying to protect the girl, she is of no concern to me. I only wanted her here because I knew it would bring you to me. You will make an excellent addition to my collection." The creature said calmly.

"If you wanted me to come over all you had to do was call, shoot me a text or hit me up on one of 5 social media sites." I say with as much attitude as I can to throw off how much I hurt.

"Oh what quick wit you have, resilient too. I hope you don't assume that little flick against the wall was my best shot." The creature said. He began to rip the cloth off of his arms and removed the cloak. I saw that the creature was slouched and squatting. It turned and postured to its full size as it faced me. It stood every bit of eight feet on legs that looked like a bulls. His large frame was covered in red glowing runes. Scaled and flesh arms reached out to its sides with massive claws.

"What and who the fuck are you?" I say, trying to hide my horror.

"I've been known by many names over the centuries I've walked on this plane. The 'what' is simple, I am a collector, and I am your destroyer." The monstrosity said, letting out a roar.

I'm not sure if it was the time or the roar but I could see Jenny starting to stir on the ground behind the beast. Jenny must have seen the massive creature, because she let out a blood curdling scream. The beast turned to see Jenny, and I reacted the only way I knew how.

I picked up an end table that was near by and threw it at the beast and yelled at the top of my lungs "RUN". Scrambling to her feet Jenny took off in a dead sprint. I had my knife in hand and was leaping onto the beast's back before I knew what I was doing.

Jenny was stopping at every door looking for anywhere that she could get away. I'm holding on and stabbing the creature, but not doing any damage. It reaches back to try to get a grip and is thrashing violently. I manage to avoid its first few attempts. I make one final stab with my blade to the side of its neck. The blade goes in a few inches just as I'm bucked off the creature, sending me toppling across the floor. Its right claw struck down and connected with my chest then drew back. As I scurry away backwards to prevent a second attempt to disembowel me, I pat myself down for blood, nothing.

Once on my feet, I race to Jenny and grab her hand and pull her to the basement door. Entering the stairwell, I look back to see the beast reaching and trying to remove my knife from his neck. The roars and thrashing causes the entire house to tremble.

Jenny and I rush down the floating bone stairs. The steps dip slightly with each bounding step. Every breath burns like lava, but I guess I can be glad my insides stayed where they belong. I can feel my broken ribs at the slightest movement, but that's the least of my problems now. We arrive at the basement floor and I pull out my flashlight so I can try to retrace my steps from earlier.

"Stay behind me. I didn't see anything down here when I broke in, but you never know." I tell Jenny as I look around.

"Fine, but when we get out of here you better explain what the fuck is going on." Jenny says in an angry tone.

"Deal, but first things first. So, do you think we can still make the show." I say, trying to get her mind away from being scared for a moment.

"What? Are you crazy?" Jenny asks as she looks back up the stairs

"Sorry, just trying to get your mind off of things." I say, trying to apologize.
"It's cool, lets just get the fuck outta here!" Jenny says in a hurried voice.

I lead the way with her close on my heels, holding on to the back of my hoodie. We move at a speed fast enough to create distance, but still able to figure out where I came in. My light dimmed like something was sucking the power from it. Sigils on the walls and ceiling brightened the room. I recognize a few of the glowing carvings from the markings on the behemoth we dealt with upstairs. Knowing this can't lead to anything good, we searched even faster.

With a thunderous crash, the basement door exploded to kindling. The vicious roar echoed down the stairwell, indicating that times almost up and round two is going to be a reality. I see the scuff marks on the floor from when I hit the ground on my clumsy landing. The wall looks solid, but in this house that doesn't always mean it is.

Jenny and I run our hands across the wall, banging every few inches to try to find a weak spot, when her hand goes right through a stone that sits about shoulder level. I rush over and tell her not to pull her hand out so it doesn't close on her.

"Step on my knee, I will give you a boost. When you get to the other side, run! Get to my apartment if you can!" I tell her frantically

"What about you?" Jenny says questioning my plan.

"Don't worry about me, I've done stupider things." I say jokingly, as I kneel down, ready to give her a boost.

With one big shove, Jenny disappears through the wall. I tap the wall and it's solid again. I have to wait till the house shifts, opening the gap again. I look back over my shoulder to see if the creature has made it down here yet, just in time to see my blade flying at my head. Ducking the blade by dropping to the ground, it barely misses me. I pick it up on the run, dodging to my left to avoid anything else this thing might want to hurl at me.

As I circled the beast I noticed he had to turn his body to see to the left from where I stabbed him in the neck. I see a bright flash and rip in the wall where Jenny went through, then a large arm come from the void. I would recognize that arm anywhere, it's Sebastian. The beast sees it as well and wants to block my escape. I take make a mad dash directly at the creature and wait till it starts to swing its massive claw. I dive to the ground to its right and slash its thigh. Rolling to my feet I grab hold of Sebastian's' massive paw and he yanks me free to the night air.

Laying there on the cool damp grass out of breath and feeling my muscles burn and bones ache. I just want to lay here and not move. I feel something grip my boot and I start sliding back towards the house. Looking down I see the beast's claw latched on. I scream and begin kicking at the claws with my other foot. Sebastian pulls a glass vial from his jacket pocket and throws it at the house, shattering it causing the fluid to splash on the exposed arm of the creature. Smoke rises from the flesh of the arm and his grip releases. We weren't going to wait to see if it would try again. Both Sebastian and I are on our feet and running. I pull him to follow me down the block just in case the beast doesn't know where I live I don't want to lead him to my doorstep.

"What was in that vile?" I say out of breath as we run.

"Holy water" Sebastian says with heaving breaths.

"Holy water, holy water! Why didn't you give me that before I went in that damned place?" I say not even bothering to look where I'm going.

"Didn't know if it would work. Figured it was worth a shot." Sebastian says with a grin.

We circle around the block and cut through the back of my apartment building and head up stairs. Most of the building is under construction and I'm one of the few living in this dump. We make our way to my door and announce that its us so Mother would know who's barging in.

Sebastian and I get inside and I lock the door. He hurries down the hallway to check on mother and I stay by the door emptying my pockets of the remaining gear. I make my way to the living room to tell mother what happened and unzip my hoodie. I'm barely around the corner when Jenny runs up and wraps her arms around me tightly.

"You made it" Jenny whispered as she her head rested on my shoulder

"Careful now, I just got tossed around by a giant. " I say with a wince

"Sorry. What the hell was that thing and what the hell were you doing there?" Jenny asked loosening her grip and taking a step back.

"First, thank you because I'm pretty sure I've got a few broke ribs. Secondly I have no clue what that was. I was hoping Mother would be able to help with that. Oh by the way this is Mother and that big hunk of man is Sebastian. And C, that last part's a long story. If you stick around I would love to try to explain." I tell her. Jenny waves hello to Mother and Sebastian.

"Sebastian how did you know where to reach through or that I would be there to be pulled out?" I asked puzzled

"I watch the girl come out from the window and Mother said you might need some help." Sebastian says as he straightening his shirt.

"Well thanks." I say still holding Jenny.

"You scream like a little girl." Sebastian chuckles.

"Did you see what grabbed me? That thing was huge!" I yelled

"Boys, enough" Mother said sharply

Sebastian and I nod yes to acknowledge Mother. Then I turn my attention back to Jenny and asks "Are you Okay, do we need to get you to the hospital or anything?" I ask concerned

" Just a little banged up, I'll be alright. I would really like to know what the hell is going on." Jenny says, sounding lost.

We sat down across from Mother and I let her explain what I am and how we knew what was going to happen. Jenny inched closer to me and examined my visible scars. After a few hours Jenny and I went off on our own to talk. Our conversation went on till morning when she noticed the sun rise.

"Shit! My phone, I need to let my friends know where I'm at." Jenny frantically said searching her pockets.

"Ummm, it's in your car." I say.

"How do you...... oh yeah you were in my head. Perv" Jenny says with a smile

"Hey it's not my fault I was in there and I promise I didn't do or see anything that would make it pervish" I reply

I carefully walk her to her car on the street, watching the house for any movement. It's silent and still which could go either way on the good bad scale. So cautious is how I will play it. Once we made it to her car she got in and fired it up. I was ready to close the door when she popped out and kissed me on the cheek. Then she slammed the door, dropped it into gear and peeled out.

"Thanks Lancelot" she yelled over the engines rumble and was out of sight.

On my way back upstairs I began unbuttoning the leather armor shirt that Sebastian gave me. It loosened back to the original size when it was fully undone. Trying to be quiet as I entered the apartment I see Mother sitting in the recliner in the living room. She waves me over and points to the chair across from her for me to sit. I look over to find Sebastian stretched out on the small couch passed out. After three days straight of standing guard I would be to I thought. I sit down and peel the armor off setting it on the floor.

"Tell me what you saw Jacob." Mother says quietly

Not knowing where to begin I describe the basement and the markings. I tell her about the smell and dampness of everything. Once I start telling her what the monstrosity looked like she raised her hand to stop me.

"Did he say anything to you?" Mother asked with a look that was worrisome.

"Yeah, he said the girl was of no concern to him, he wanted me, he has many names and he was some sort of collector. Why do you know who this thing is? I tell her.

"I was afraid this day would come." Mother says lowering her head.

"Well who is he and what day is that?" I say getting antsy

"It's name is Akhkharu, it is from an ancient Sumerian word meaning roughly vampire or the Darkness." Mother says hesitantly.

"Vampire, really? That didn't look like any vampire I've ever heard of" I say
"Not vampire like in the movies or TV. Those are bastardized versions of some fools imagination. Akhkharu is a devourer of souls. He collects his victims souls and attributes for uses as his own." Mother explains

"So you're telling me he wants me for the curse that I ended up with." I say with my hand on my chest in disbelief.

"That so called curse saved Jenny's life last night. Think about what something could do with it once they harness the power. It would allow them to control anyone they want and supply him with a never ending buffet of souls. With every soul he grows stronger." Mother says thinking of her own fate.

"How do you know so much about this Ak-whatever?" I ask

"He has hunted our kind since before written time. Most can stay hidden and avoid coming across the ones that hunt us or want to use our gift for their own needs." Mother tells me.

"This is a lot to process right now. I need sleep." I say trying not to yawn

"Get some rest dear boy, we will talk more when you wake." Mother says in a soft tone
"Cool, but not before I get my coffee. Good night or morning whatever" I say and then walk to my room and fall on the bed.

I wake up to the smell of coffee and food in the other room. After convincing my body to sit up right I realize I must have been more tired than I thought. I scoot to the end of the bed and lean forward till I reach the door and swing it closed. I take off my boots and examine the right one. The claw marks were deep enough to cut through the leather and scratch the steel tip underneath. Tossing them to the side I begin digging through a pile of laundry next to the bed for something clean to wear, or something that doesn't smell like a foot. I find some cargo pants and a shirt from a band called Dark Apostle that was tossed to me while I stood outside a metal show. I don't think I've ever worn it but it's clean. I stagger from my room to see the sun beaming in the window like a searchlight. Half blind I glance around the room and see Sebastian had pulled a chair near the window to keep watch. I head towards the kitchen and am met by Mother. She was holding a plate piled high with food.

"For me, thanks" I say reaching for the plate.

"Get your own, this is for Sebastian. He need to keep watch." Mother says passing the food to Sebastian.

"Well hell, I hope you made enough for me at least." I say as I stagger around, trying to wake up.

"I didn't make anything" Mother says and pointed around the corner.

I walk around to the kitchen to see Jenny by the stove. She has headphones on and doesn't notice me watching her. "How long has she been here?" I ask mother

"Only about 45 minutes or so." Mother says

I walk over to tap Jenny on the shoulder so I'm not stuck standing there with like a whack job and the smell of the food is making me even hungrier. I get within two feet when she turns and startled spills coffee on me.

"Sorry, I didn't know you were there." Jenny says still holding the cup

"It's cool, these clothes were too clean anyways." I say trying to make her feel better

"Well that's what you get for sneaking up on people. I hope you learned your lesson" Jenny says with a smile

"Sure did, next time I will be more careful." I tell her returning her smile with one of my own.
"You better. Now clean up your mess" She says and tosses me a rag to dry off.

Kneeling on the floor I start wiping up the coffee. I look up at her and say "Not trying to be rude, but what are you doing here? I figured you would be home resting and recovering from it all."

"Well if you must know, you weren't answering my calls or text so I was trying to see if you were still alive or avoiding me." Jenny says crossing her arms and leaning against the counter.

"I must have had my phone on vibrant and slept right through it." I say looking for my phone.

I find it on the end table. Once I unlock the screen I notice that there were 18 missed calls and 17 text messages waiting. "Wow that's a lot of missed calls for just a short time." I say

"Short time, short time. No a short time would be if that was one day." Jenny says seeming disturbed by what I said.

"What are you talking about? I just saw you a few hours ago." I say confused

Mother walks up and places her hand on my shoulder. Jenny points to her and says "would you tell him or do you want me to"
"What is she talking about, tell me what?" I ask mother.
"Child, I don't know how to break it to you but you've been asleep for 4 days. It's Wednesday afternoon." Mother says calmly

"4 days, you let me sleep for 4 days!" I say trying to not raise my voice.

"Yes, we tried to wake you but you wouldn't come to. So we've been watching over you to make sure you would come out of it." Mother says

"Wait a minute, I don't remember giving you my number." I say looking at Jenny

"You didn't, I got it off of one of the orders you made. Don't look at me like I'm the crazy one Mr. I'm going to take a ride in your brain" Jenny says making a plate of food.

"I never said crazy, a little stalkerish but never crazy." I say jokingly as I step closer with my arms reached out trying to hug her.

"You need your strength, eat up" Jenny says jamming a plate in my hands. "plus you got coffee all over yourself."
I take my plate and walk to the living room to sit and eat. Mother waves me over to sit near her. "Come Jacob, let me tell you how this all began. I think it's time for you to know more of our kind" Mother says.

I drag my chair closer to the recliner so we can talk. Jenny comes over with her own chair so she doesn't miss anything. I sit and dig into my food, devouring it like a rabid dog. Jenny laughs and I give her a thumbs up.

"Great food, I think I'm going to have to keep you around." I say with a mouthful of biscuits and gravy.

"Don't think it's going to be that easy. You're going to have to work for it. I figured cooking for you was the least I could do to say thanks for not letting that thing kill me." Jenny says

"What the hell happened and why was I out for so long?" I say looking at Mother

"From what I can tell, the house and Akhkharu are connected. It's been dormant since you got away. It might have been a spell to drain you and make you easier to trap. The bags that you buried around the yard helped lessen the spell." Mother explains

"So what do you know of this Akhkharu, you said you can tell me how all of this madness began" I say as I get up to take my plate to the kitchen. Jenny stops me and takes my plate for me. I give her a silent thank you. Once back from the kitchen jenny gets back in her spot appearing like a 5 year old ready for story time.

"This is how it was told to me, this story is not written down but passed down from generation to generation. In ancient Sumeria the old gods ruled over all. As time passed they became tired of the way things were. The decision was made to grant special skills or abilities to the leaders of the different sects of people. One sect leader received the power over the elements, one has......" I stop Mother

"Wait are you saying that there's more freaks out there like us?" I question

"Just listen and you will learn. Also I am one of those so called freaks, and I don't like that term." Mother says. I raise my hand to apologize and to tell her to continue.

"Okay, where was I before I was so rudely interrupted. Oh yes, one over the elements, one having the power over the mind that would be us, you just need to practice and it will come to you, one sect leader could live as an immortal, one leader was granted mystical powers, one was give unbreakable strength. Over time the leaders tried to produce offspring with other sects to try to create the perfect ruler. They wanted to join forces to take the power back and rule themselves. All this did was dilute the powers and form bastardized versions of the once great leaders. Driving many of them mad trying to control their powers. Some sects stayed away to keep a level of purity in the bloodline. There were a few of the lesser gods that took offense to these gifts and what man was doing with them. That's where Akhkharu comes in." Mother says stopping as Jenny gets up.

"Sorry to dine and dash but I got to get to work or I'll be late. Turn your ringer on and I'll give you a call later." Jenny says grabbing her stuff.

I grab my phone and turn the volume up and plug it in so it could charge. "volume is up, phone charging and I will be eagerly waiting for your call." I say in a smartass tone

"Keep it up and you won't get any free food tonight" Jenny snaps back at me. Just then I get hit with a pillow that seemed to come out of nowhere.
"Shut your mouth boy, I want a calzone." Says Sebastian as he sits looking out the window.

"Dude, I forgot you were even here." I say

"As I was saying.." mother said pointing at Sebastian and I. "this is where Akhkharu comes in. He was not happy with how the mortals were misusing these gifts. He also wasn't happy that such gifts were bestowed upon a lower form of life than himself. Akhkharu was the collector of souls. He has the gift to absorb souls of the average mortals as an offering to the upper gods. After scheming and planning it's said that he convinced the old gods to give him the ability to retrieve the abilities that were given to the sect leaders if they were misused so he could deliver them back to his master. After returning a few of the abilities to his masters he began to consume them for himself making him more powerful. With each soul observed and each new skill gained he tried to overthrow the old gods. This caused him to be banished to walk the earth in his twisted form driven mad with a hunger that cannot be quenched. Akhkharu has been hunting our kind along with the remaining gifted of the other sects ever since." Mother says

"Holy hell, how many of the gifted ones are left out there?" I ask

"There is no way to know for sure. Most have scattered to the wind and gone into hiding to avoid his wrath." Mother says

"Why here, why now?" I ask

"Well there's a high concentration of gifted in this area. I know of five in this city alone, but only four of them know the possess an ability." Mother says looking at the dormant house out the window from her chair.

"I know there's me and you, that's two. Who are the others and are they like us? Like us I mean hitchhikers." I say stumbling over my words in confused amazement

"No, not like us, other abilities and as for who that's not for me to say." Mother said with what seemed like the weight of the world on her shoulders. "they will tell you when they are ready if they want to share in their secret"

"I understand. Well if they do maybe they are willing to help so they no longer have to hide." I say throwing the idea out there.

"Enough of that for now, let me check your wounds. You will be no good to any of us if you are too weak to take care of yourself." Mother says waving me in front of her

I remove my shirt so she can peal the bandages off. The bandages were soaked through will dried blood from not changing it for the past four days. Mother gets a wet dish cloth from the kitchen then starts peeling the tape wetting the edges. Every time I look down to see how it's going mother pushes my head out of the way. Once the side and bottom were off she pulled it back slowly, wiping the damp towel to release the bandage from the skin. I can feel the pulling as it sticks on my tender flesh. Mothers momentum increased and the wiping became more feverish. I was starting to get worried because out of the corner of my eye I could see her look of confusion as she scrubbed.

"Sebastian come look at this and tell me what you see" Mother demands

Sebastian got up from his post and hurried to see what was so urgent. Sebastian stood there staring at my shoulder where Akhkharu had clawed me while in Jenny's head. I felt him running his massive fingers over the area. I start to try and turn my head and mother blocks it before I can get it halfway.

"Either let me look or tell me what is going on!" I snap

"Tell me Jacob, how many scars would you say were there before you were mauled?" Mother asks me

"I don't know, 4 or 5. I didn't really keep track why?" I say

"Take of look for yourself" Mother says with a hint of worry in her voice

I rush to the hallway to get a look in the mirror and see what was so concerning. Where there was once a mix of scars from past horrors and the bleeding claw marks from Akhkharu was now a shimmering onyx colored skin. I run my fingers through the grooves of the stone like scarring. The area is smooth as glass but feels thicker and more durable. I move my arm and shrug my shoulder and it has the freedom of movement like normal skin.

I turn to run back to Mother for an explanation but find her and Sebastian standing at the edge of the hall looking awestruck. "What is this, what's happening to me?"

"I don't know Jacob but I will find out what I can from a few who might know. Until then try to stay calm. We have other things to worry about." Mother says in a calming voice shoeing Sebastian back to his post.

I stood in front of the mirror for long while looking over the transformation of the exposed flesh from the attack. I decided to try and clear my head with the only thing I could think of, manual labor. I haven't done any actual work on renovations of this dump in a week and figured if I don't show some progress to the owner I would be out on my ass. I throw on my shirt and grabbed my tool belt and headed to where I had left off. I told mother to call my cell if she needed me to rush back. This work was a distraction and was helping for a while. I started thinking of what would happen if Akhkharu decided to come over here and it brought up more questions that changed my mind on what needs fixed first.

Looking at my supplies I made a list of things that needed to be reinforced to prevent a direct assault on my place. I figured out a few locations that traps could be set as well. Maybe I've watched a few too many movies but it's all I really had to go on. I've never found a book or website that was titled how to protect your home from a lesser god attack, so winging it is the best I got.

I remember my knife seemed to slow him down some and it looked as if the holy water burned the shit out of him so I need to stock up on those things. Knives are easy enough to get, hell I could make a few with all the scrap metal around here and my old grinder. The holy water is another issue.

I'm not sure if I'm going to be able to find it at the store by the gallon and the churches don't have enough sitting out to just walk in and snatch it. I need to check with Sebastian and see where he got that bottle he had of it.

My phone rings so I pull it out of my pocket and check the caller ID, it's Jenny. "Hey, what's going on?" I say

"Not much, just getting off work." Jenny says

"Short day?" I ask

"No, I put in a full 8. Seeing if you wanted me to stop by. There's a show tonight and thought you might want to go and get away for a bit" Jenny says

"8 hours, well Okay then I guess I lost track of time. Yeah sure come on over I will get cleaned up some. I'm covered in sheet rock dust at the moment" I tell her

"Okay, see you in a few, tell Mother and Sebastian I got them some grub." Jenny says
"Will do, bye" I say then hang up.
I head back to the apartment to try to find clean clothes to go out in when it hits me. I'm probably going to have to meet her friends.

This should be interesting but at least I will get to see some metal. I let the others know Jenny is on the way over with food for them and we might go watch a few bands play when I hear a loud crash come from the stairs.

"What was that?" Sebastian said popping out of his chair

"Jacob, you son of a bitch. Get out here!" Jenny yells

"Oh shit, coming" I yell back as I run for the door. I see Jenny standing on the stairs with one foot buried through the step.

"Sorry, I should have told you to take the back stairs. I was doing some remodeling after you left and got distracted" I say helping her get her foot unstuck.

"Distracted, what could've distracted you enough to make you forget that you took boards off the steps in an area that never has proper lighting?" Jenny asked with fury.

"Well you called as I was changing the lightbulbs" I say as I get her foot free

"Oh, well I can see that. But I'm afraid the food might be a little flatter than normal." She says looking at the bag of food.

We pick everything up and head inside so I can finish getting ready. I set the food on the table. Mother looks at the squashed boxes and back at me.

"The food broke my fall, sorry" Jenny says to Mother

"It will be Okay child, it's Jacob's fault anyway." Mother says giving me an evil look.

I grab the leather armor of the back of the chair and head in the bedroom to finish getting dressed. I get my pants and boots on when jenny pops her head in the door and sees me with no shirt.

"I didn't realize you had so many scars" Jenny says sadly. "Do you remember how they all happened?"

"Not all of them. I was really young when they started showing up" I tell her grabbing the armor off the bed to put on.

She stops before I get both arms in to examine my newest addition. "is this from the other night when you were in my head?" she asks

"Yeah, I never thought to ask. How is your shoulder?" I ask realizing that if I got hurt this bad she should be cut up as well.

"I'm fine, didn't even break the skin" she says pulling the collar of her shirt over to show me. "Why is yours all black and smooth?"

"I have no clue, Mother is checking in on that." I say pulling the armor on and buttoning it up. "Let me get a shirt on and we can get out of here." I grab a shirt from the pile and put it on. Most of my shirts are long sleeve. It saves time explaining the scars to people plus it covers up the armor. I'm still a little self-conscious about them.

We head out to the living room so I can grab my phone before we leave. Sebastian already has one calzone finished and working on his second. Mother is taking her time with hers.

"So where are you two off to this late at night?" Mother asks being nosy.

"There's a midnight metal night going on at a club not far from here. Just a couple local bands playing" Jenny says

"Sounds fun, well at least you're getting him out of the house for a change. He needs to interact with people. Less of a chance he breaks anything else around this place." Mother jokes " go on get out of here we will let you know if there's any changes"

"Well with that being said to make me sound like a homely pathetic loser I think we will lead out" I say with the amazed feeling that I got burned and called out by mother.

Sebastian never taking his eyes of the window waves bye. I'm thinking it was more to Jenny than for me. We take the back stairs out of the building and follow the alley to the front to Jenny's car but she keeps walking down the sidewalk.

"We can hoof it from here it's only a few block. It will give us a chance to talk before it's too loud." Jenny says

"Works for me, what do you want to talk about?" I ask

"Well I don't know too much about you but it seems we have some kind of a connection. So tell me some stuff." Jenny says looping her arm in mine.

"Not too much to tell really. Most of this stuff is new to me. Mother has been helping me learn how to control it better and before I meet her I was in and out of state custody. Everything from foster care to state hospitals." I tell her

"Well how did you meet Mother and what's Sebastian's deal?" Jenny asked

"Long story short, mother found me. She sent Sebastian to grab me and take me to her when I went to a psychic fair a while back. As for Sebastian, I don't know much about him. He doesn't talk much, well not around me. For all I know he's up there now being a regular chatty Cathy." I say

"That's good that you guys met up. At least you have somebody to help you and not have to figure it all out on your own." Jenny says

"Yeah, mother has been a big help. What did you tell your friends about what happened?" I ask

"That you kidnapped me and now I'm suffering from Stockholm syndrome." She says smiling ear to ear.
"God I hope you are joking, this is going to be awkward enough as it is." I say wondering
We walk quietly for a few blocks, her arm entwined with mine. To the unknowing passers-by it would appear like we are a couple and never know we just met a week ago, nor will they have the slightest idea that an ancient lesser god type creature attacked her to get to me.

Trying to break the awkward silence we had going on I say "You didn't really tell your friends that did you, I mean I don't want them to hate me already."

"Calm down there, Scarface. Everything will be fine. You need to loosen up a little." Jenny says pulling me closer. "If I say you're good people you will be Okay with them."

"I hope you are right, and what the fuck? Scarface, really? You're going to give me a complex or something. Maybe therapy, who know." I say noticing the club up ahead.

"Oh you need therapy but that's not my fault." Jenny laughs

She unlinks her arm and grabs my hand pulling me to the front of the line. The door guy sees it her and waves us in. Once inside, the crowd is overwhelming with everyone crowding the circle bar by the door. For once I'm glad for poor lighting and alcohol. We make it no more than five feet in when we get separated by her friends rushing past me to get to Jenny. While they say their hellos I slowly worm my way to the bar. I manage to get the bartender's attention by holding up a twenty dollar bill and signal I need four beers. I grab my drinks and tell him to keep the change. I'm halfway through the first beer when Jenny runs up.

"Sweet, you got us drinks" Jenny said as she started passing them out to her friends.

I lean over and say quietly in her ear so the others don't hear "actually those were all mine. I didn't know what you wanted and you seemed to busy to ask."

"Oh don't be that way" Jenny says pouting

"What way?" I say

She gives me a look that I've seen from Mother when I'm picking on Sebastian and say "these are my friends. This is Louis, Jody and Sarah. Louis plays in one of the bands tonight. Everyone this is my kidnapper Jacob."

Shaking everyone's hand I say "I didn't really kidnap her, she's just mad that I lived inside her head for a short time." They just kind of stood there for a moment confused.

"So who's playing next?" Jenny asked trying to change the subject.

"It's going to be Rimjob, Thy Abandonment, and Torn the Fuck Apart" Louis says motioning that he wanted to head towards the stage.

Jenny must have noticed me getting nervous and anxious with everything going on around me because she leaned over when the others started making their way to the front and whispered in my ear "Calm down, I'm not going anywhere. You think after fighting a god, meeting my friends would be a piece of cake"

"I don't like cake" I say back to her. She smiles and kisses my cheek then drags me to the stage area where the band is setting up.

"Karl!" Jenny yells

"What do you want woman?" Karl says as he's trying to help with the drum kit.

"Hurry up, I got someone I want you to meet." Jenny says to Karl over the blaring of the house music.

While the band is doing sound check and getting everything set up Jenny tells me to stay put and pulls Sarah to the side. I can't tell what they are saying but I know they are talking about me from the looks I keep getting from the both of them. I can only imagine what she's telling her, knowing what the truth is Sarah could think she's joking. Hell if I wasn't there I probably wouldn't believe it either. Out of the corner of my eye I see someone staring at me. I turn to look and the guy looks away. Thinking I might be a bit paranoid I brush it off. Karl sets his microphone back on the stand and hops down off the stage and walks over to Jenny.

Jenny waves for me to come over for I assume another introduction. I hold up my hand for her to give me a second and grab a few shots from the side bar before heading over. If I would have thought I would be buying so many drinks I would've brought more cash. I walk up with a two handfuls of shots and pass them around keeping 2 for myself.

"I'm guessing you're Karl. I'm Jacob, Jenny's kidnapper." I say with a grin.

"That's cool, I tried it once myself but she's too needy to keep around the house for any longer than a day or two." Karl said as Jenny punches him in the arm

"She's violent as well" I say preparing to get hit as well

Jenny grabbed my shirt and pulled me over to her and said "You like it and you know it"

Karl sees someone waving for him from the corner of the stage at him and says "that's Fred telling me to hurry. I got to get ready, we go in in five"

While Karl headed to the room to get ready I scanned the room. The shots were starting to work and I was getting less antsy and starting to relax. If two helped a little maybe two more would do wonders. Jenny is talking to Sarah and Jody and I motion that I'm going to hit the bar if anyone wants another. Jenny smiles and nods her head yes. So I make my way to the bar and see the guy that was watching me earlier standing to my left.

"How's it going?" I ask

"Going okay I guess, what about you?" the man says

"Not too bad, never heard these bands before. Kinda excited to see what they're like." I say

"All the bands tonight are good. It's a good mix of black metal, death and gutter grind. New to the area?" the man says then takes a drink.

While he was taking a drink I see the what looks like a rune tattooed on his right wrist. I turn more towards him after I order my drinks and see another behind his ear. This could be a coincidence with most of the people here having tattoos but I doubt it. So I try to steer the conversation in a different direction.

"Yeah, I lived up in Seattle for a while but after I got back from overseas I felt it was time to start fresh. My squad got hit with an IED while out on maneuvers. I spent so much time in a medical unit healing up I wanted to go somewhere new and experience life." I say

"That's cool, I guess that explains the scars then." The man says

"Yeah they bother most people. I like your ink." I say as I try to get a closer look at the tattoos.

"Hey I got to get back to my friends, enjoy the show" the man says as he walks off

I down a shot at the bar and head back to Jenny and her friends.

"Here you go ladies, hey do you know that guy?" I ask Jenny, pointing the guy out

"I've seen him around but I wouldn't say I know him." Jenny says

"He's friends with Fred, I don't think I've ever got his name. Kind of cute though." Sarah says

"Why do you ask?" Jenny asked

"No reason, he was looking at me for a while is all." I say

"Probably because you were talking to Karl." Sarah says

"That explains it, no worries. Lets watch some metal and have a good time." I say

The lights went down and Jenny points for me to watch as Rimjob takes the stage. First out is Fred wearing a thong, tube top and baby doll mask. Then I see Karl walk out wearing a bow tie and bubble wrap smeared petroleum jelly.

The others walk out in various outfits equally disturbing and start playing. During the set I see free take off his tube top and toss it to the crowd. When he stood up I can see what look like more runes matching the ones on the basement wall of that house and the torso of Akhkharu.

Trying to act normal so I don't worry Jenny, I continue head banging along with the music. The set went on for about 30 minutes or so before they were done. The band start tearing down their gear and I tell Jenny I will be right back. I have to ask Fred about those tattoos. I wait by the stage as they go in and out the door with equipment. One band setting up while Rimjob gets their stuff off stage. I follow Karl outside with a cabinet to see if Fred is there.

"Hey have you seen Fred, I wanted to let him know what I thought of the set?" I ask Karl

He looks around for a minute and says "He was just here a minute ago, but I don't see his truck any more."

"Well shit, you did great let him know for me." I say

I head back in just in time for Thy Abandonment to take stage. I look around the room and spot jenny, Jody and Sarah standing on the left side of stage. As I make my way over I try to find the guy I was chatting up earlier at the bar but he's nowhere to be found.

"Where'd you run off to?" Jenny asks playfully

"I was helping Karl with the gear, where did your friend Louis disappear to?" I say looking around.

She turns my head towards the stage and I see him standing a few feet away. I hardly recognized him with the change of clothes and corpse paint. I shake my head in acknowledgment and take a drink of my beer. The show continued and the other bands killed it. The club was clearing out and people saying goodbyes as they made their way to their vehicles to head home. Jenny and I waited outside for a few minutes with Jody and Sarah while they waited on Louis to settle his bar tab.

Once the three of them leave Jenny and I head back to my apartment. Jenny leans on my shoulder as we walk. I'm fighting the urge to tell her my thoughts about Fred and his friend so I hold off till I talk to mother. I reassure her that I had a good time so she doesn't feel bad or concerned over nothing. I'm not too use to this relationship thing, hell I don't even know if that's what this is. We walk arm and arm for a few blocks and it's strange to me being able to be myself around someone that isn't off put my the scars or my past.

We make it to Jenny's car and I hesitate not sure if I should ask her up or send her home for the night. With mother and Sebastian upstairs there's not much privacy so I cancel that idea.

"I would ask you up for a nightcap but there's two people up there that are probably watching us as we speak." I say

"It's okay, I got tomorrow or today or whatever it is off so I will swing by once I get my beauty sleep." Jenny says fidgeting with the string of my hoodie.

"Sounds good to me. Text me when you get home so I know you made it safe" I tell her

"Awe you really do care don't you? You know I will" Jenny says with a huge grin
She hops in the car and fires the 80's muscle up with a rev of the engine. I lean inside and try to kiss her cheek to say goodbye as she turns her head causing our lips to meet.

"Trying to sneak a kiss are you?" Jenny asks

"Hey you turned your head so that's on you. I wouldn't say I didn't enjoy it but I'm innocent on that one" I say smiling

I stand back up right and she gets out of the car and grabs my head and kisses me. I slide my arms around her back to hold her as we kiss. Time seems to stop and I feel like I'm both in my head and hers at the same moment in time and space. When we pulled apart there was a moment when all was in a haze and from her reaction she had felt it as well. Without another word spoken Jenny got in her car and drove off. I stood watching the taillights of the Camaro get further away until they were out of sight.

I ventured to the alley on the side of my rundown apartment building to make my way to the rear stairs. Things seemed quiet and I had almost forgotten what I was going to tell mother. Getting to my door I opened it without thinking. It occurred to me that with everything going on they should have had It locked up tight and not left unsecured.

"Mother? Sebastian? Hello, why's the door unlocked?" I yell as I walk down the hallway. After I didn't get an answer I slowly started searching the apartment room by room. Halfway through my place I realize that nobody is here and with the way I keep the place I couldn't tell if there was a struggle or not.

In the kitchen I grab the pizza box sitting on the counter and flip it open to see if there's anything to eat. Inside the box there's 2 pieces of pizza and a note. The note says "Jacob, we had to go to follow up on some information we were looking for. We felt you might need the place guest free for the night. Mother". Well being to wired to sleep after a four day coma means I've got some time to myself. I grabbed some paper and a pencil so I can draw out the tattoos that I saw on that guy Fred and his friend. Maybe mother will know something about the meaning behind each one. I text Sebastian to let him know that I might have a lead and to call when they can.

The sun comes and burns my eyes catching me off guard since I must have dozed off at some point reading these old books Mother left here. I check my phone only to find no messages or missed calls. I scrounge through the fridge for something to eat and see if I have any coffee left, nothing.

With the world crashing down around me with all the information that got dropped on my lap recently I completely forgot the little things like groceries and laundry. Still in the same clothes from the previous night's activities I grab my hoodie and head to the gas station in search of caffeine and something to stop my stomach from sounding like it's a rabid T-Rex. I walk in to find Jessie back in the kitchen area of the store. I gave Jessie the injured in combat story a while back and he takes care of me extra well since then.

"Hey Jacob, it's been a while. Do you want the usual?" Jessie asks

"Yes, but make it extra strong today. I feel like it's going to be one of those days." I tell him

"You got it, be up in a minute" Jessie says turning to grab a cup for my drink.

I search the racks for food but I know the only thing that will cure this hunger is meat and a lot of it. I'm not finding anything appetizing so I guess the coffee will have to do for now. Jessie waves me over holding my coffee up so I can see it's ready.

"I threw in 4 shots, much more and it might give you a heart attack. Hope that works for you?" Jessie says handing me the large, steaming concoction.

"Hell yes, now to find food. Thanks" I say scanning the shelves.

"No problem...... oh here, try one of these. Its double bacon, egg and cheese. Someone else ordered it and left without taking their food." Jessie says

"There is no greater sound than double bacon right now." I tell him taking the sandwich.

I pay and head to door waving to Jessie as thanks for the hook up. A block away from the apartment and the angry sounds coming from my gut have subsided and the coffee seems to be doing its job when my phone goes off. I take it out of my pocket and see it's Sebastian.

"Sebastian, what's up?" I ask after I take a sip of my drink.

"Jacob it's Mother. You sound awfully alert for this hour." Mother says

"Oh hey, yeah I just downed more caffeine than one should be allowed in a week. I have a few things I needed to tell you, when am I going to see you next?" I ask.

"Well we will let you know when we get back. It should only be a few days." Mother says over some loud background noises.

"Days? Where the hell are you and what's all that noise in the background?" I ask

"We had to go where all of this started." Mother said cryptically

"And that means what exactly?" I ask confused

"Don't worry about it, just keep your head down and I will explain everything upon our return." Mother said

"Alright fine, I know how to take a hint. Have fun and see you in a few days." I say hanging up the phone.

On my walk back to the apartment I text Jenny to see what she had going on for the day. With my newly acquired free time I decide I should catch up on some of the work that I've avoided. It will help pass the time and keep me occupied. I realize that I've never really had anyone there for or with me and now that they are away it seems odd. I even miss Sebastian a little.

My mind starts to wonder and I drift off into my own world while I'm working. I have my headphones in with the music on random when I get tapped on my shoulder by the building owner. I spin around so fast without thinking I didn't even notice I had my five pound sledge up ready to bash in whatever threat that might appear.

"Jacob, what the ever-loving hell are you doing?" Tim the apartment owner said

"Sorry bossman, you caught me off-guard. There were some squatters that I ran off the other day that said they would be back." I said

"Oh okay, well good work. Hey I'm going to be showing one of the finished apartments to some potential tenants in about 20. So can you knock off the banging for about an hour or so till they leave?" Tim asked

"Yeah sure. It's about time for a break anyway." I said

"Great, I'll text you with an all clear when you can get back to it." Tim said

"Cool, I will get out of your hair. Oh, show they 3D. It's all cleaned up and ready. I moved some of the furniture that was left when that old woman in 2A died." I say putting my tools away

"Furnished means I can charge more, good thinking." Tim says

I really wasn't hungry, so while I waited for the them to be done looking I hit the books again. Kind of curious of who would want to leave in this place I move the chair by the window as I scan some of the research material. I watch a truck pull up outside and two people get out. I can't tell what they look like from my position because they are wearing hoodies. They stop and look at the house across the street for a moment till I see Tim walk up to them.

They shake hands and head in the door. I hear them making their way up the stairs so I head down my hallway to see if I could hear anything they are saying. I can hear Tim telling them that there's an on-site maintenance person. He says that the building is under renovations but there are a few units ready to go. He tries to take them up to the third floor but they stop him.

"Are any of these on this floor ready to rent?" one man said

"Not at this time, the only one that is livable is this one and the maintenance man lives there. If you get one of the open ones on the third floor for now, you can take one of these when it's done." Tim said

"How long do you think that will be?" the other man said

"A month or so, or you could wait if you aren't in a hurry." Tim said

"We can look at the third floor first and decide from there." The first guy said

Something about the man's voice sounds familiar but I can't think of from where. I don't deal with too many people so I hope it comes to me before it's too late. Every word he says sends a shiver down my spine like I should know but I don't. Then I hear a sentence that hits me hard.

"The reason we want one on a lower floor is because he plays drums and we didn't want to haul them up that many floors every few days." The first guy said

They head up to the third floor and stay up there for about 30 minutes. While they are up stairs my heart is pounding and I'm having a hard time breathing. What are they doing here? What are they planning? The fear setting in and my brain trying to rationalize it to calm down that I might be wrong. They head out the front door and Tim heads to his office on the first floor. They stand there by the truck for a minute and turn towards my window and take off their hoods. I can see clearly now that it's Fred and his friend. They smile, wave and get in the truck and leave.

So many questions flood me sending my mind into a panic. How long have they known about me? Who sent them? Are they the only two or are there more? If they know about me they must know I'm involved with Jenny. Shit she hasn't text me back or called. I hope she's alright and they didn't do anything to her. I need to check on her but I have no clue where she lives. It comes to me, the realization that I can call her work.

I call the restaurant to see if she's working and am told she called in sick and she isn't on the schedule till Sunday. I thank the person on the phone and hang up. Feeling lost I head down to check with Tim to see if I can get any information on the guys looking at renting the apartment.

"So what's the deal with those guys, boss?" I ask as casual as possible

"I think they are going to take the place, but won't know for sure until they get the paperwork filled out. They also said they might have a few friends that were looking for new places." Tim said

"So looks like I'm going to need to get busy. How many units are you talking about needing ready and how fast?" I ask

"At least 3, and as soon as you can get them knocked out. One two bedroom and two of the three bedrooms." Tim explained

"I'm going to make a supply run then. I'm going to snag the flat bed so I can get the big stuff if you don't mind?" I say

"Do what you have to to to get them ready. This way we can get some money rolling in." Tim said tossing me the keys to the old flatbed truck.

I catch the keys and give Tim a thumbs up as I head out the door. Maybe a drive will help me think, I can't hurt. I use my phone to try to see if there are any occult stores or anything that might deal with that type stuff. A few pop up and I map a route to all of them.

One at a time I stop and look finding nothing useful until I come to one call the Urban Occultist. This one stood out to me because it wasn't all new and shinny or filled with weekend Wiccans and hipsters. Clearly these people watched Charmed too many times. This place was old and gritty with only half the letters on the sign working.

Upon entering I feel something different about the place. A quietness about the people that gave me an uneasy and off balance feeling that was making me sick to my stomach. Not one single person would look towards me as the pain grew more intense. I braced myself on the counter just inside the door and couldn't move any further. An older woman came to my side and draped a string necklace holding a medallion over my head. The very moment the charm came to rest on my neck the pain and sickness left me.

She leaned close to my ear and whispered "Mother said you would eventually find your way into my shop."

"You know Mother?" I said quietly

"Very well, we go back longer than either of us remember. My name is Jacqueline." She said

"That's fantastic and everything but what the hell was that shit when I walked in?" I said

"Lower your voice please and follow me. I believe I can explain in the back room." She said keeping her voice so low I could barely hear the words.

"Outstanding, another meeting in a backroom. Lead the way." I whisper

After what happened just a few minutes ago at the entrance I pull my hood up hoping nobody would see my face. The last thing I need is to have any of those rune wearing weirdos know what can cripple me. As I follow Jacqueline through the maze of cluttered shelves and dust covered display cases I realize that every person in this store was avoiding me like the plaque. They seemed aware of my presence and avoided eye contact and moved out of our way with a purpose. It seemed more like fear than avoidance, carefully keeping their backs turned toward me. We walk through a curtain at the rear of the shop away from onlookers and Jacqueline stops me once the curtain falls into its resting location.

"You won't need the medallion any longer, but you are welcome to keep it." Jacqueline says

"I think I might just hang onto it for now. What the hell was that back there?" I say

"I know you have questions and we will get to that. We can speak freely back here." Jacqueline says

"Peachy, now why the hell did it feel like I wanted to die when I walked in this place?" I ask

"The entryway is made from the Rowan tree. This keeps all supernatural or those other than humans at bay. And that medallion I gave you nullified the effects on the wearer." Jacqueline says

"So you are saying I'm either supernatural or non-human. That's just freaking great. One more thing to add to my resume." I say throwing my hands up

"You are special that's for sure. I've never seen something make it all the way inside before. Every other gifted gets stopped before they touch the door. Mother said you were different." Jacqueline says

"So what's the deal with your customers? They seemed kinda special themselves." I say

"They are regulars here, non-gifted that come here to learn. They know the rules and properties of the Rowan tree. What you did walking right through probably scared them and they didn't want to anger something that could break through." Jacqueline tells me.

"I'm trying to find some information about some runes. I can't find anything with the limited resources I have." I say

"Stay here, I believe I have a book at the front that might help." Jacqueline says

Jacqueline leaves through the curtain heading to get the book. I walk around the room looking around the room. I examine the shelves, scrolling the titles of books. Some titles were easy to make out, others were in languages I won't even attempt. Along the wall, cases held glass jars filled with various animal parts, plants, powders, liquids and what I can only describe as oddly colored smokes. My attention is caught by a Tesla coil arcing in the corner. I reach for it and I hear footsteps nearing the doorway. Jacqueline enters the room with both arms full of books and rolled up parchment.

"Please stay away from that. The things in this room are not toys." Jacqueline says

"Fine." I mumble

"Come help me with these please, or clear a spot on the table." Jacqueline says

I head over to the table and start stacking books to one side. I set a few of the boxes on the floor and take a few of the scrolls out of her hands. She sets the remaining items down and begins sorting them out.

While Jacqueline sorted her books I continued checking out all the dust covered objects in the room. Most things look like they haven't been moved or touched in decades from the amount of build up. I came across an area that was somewhat clean. There was a tarp covering something on top of a small display case. Why is this the only clean stuff back here. What is so important with it and what is being hidden. The curiosity was driving me nuts. I had to find out.

"Get away from that and start going through some of this." Jacqueline snapped at Jacob

"What's under this tarp?" I ask

"Don't worry about that right now, there will be plenty of time to browse later" she said

"Alright, alright. Where do you think I need to start?" I ask

"Start with this one. It discusses sigils and their meaning. Then move on to this one, it's about runes." She says sliding two massive books my direction.

Hours went by as we scoured through the tower of script with little to no luck. For all I know it could've been right in front of my face and I wouldn't have known. I wasn't even sure what I needed to be looking for to begin with and over half of this crap isn't even in English and a few were just symbols. Time seemed to not exist in this room. Thinking that by the time I find something I'm going to have a layer of dust to brush off before leaving my mind wanders to Jenny. There's been no calls or text causing the worst possible outcomes to scroll through like the bad B-Movie marathon at the drive-in. I try to focus and see something that looks familiar in a picture dated 392 A.D.

"Hey check this out!" I say louder than expected. After no answer I look up and see that Jacqueline wasn't even in the room. I get up and head to the curtain to the main store. I've grown stiff from sitting for so long and stretch and pull my hood up so I don't freak out the normal customers and step through. The place looks closed with the lights off and shades drawn on the front windows. There a dim light showing in a doorway behind the register. I approach the door slowly not knowing what I will find. I yell out Jacqueline's name as I creep closer.

"I'll be right there doll, just head back to the room and I'll bring refreshments " Jacqueline yells back.

"Okay, I found something you should see." I say

I stand still for a moment thinking she might need help carrying stuff again. I hear what sounds like low whispering barely audible if it weren't for that being the only sound in the place. I quietly step closer to the door and I hear Jacqueline speaking to someone.

"I need to get back to this customer, I trust you can show yourself out the same way you came in." Jacqueline whispers

There was no answer in response only the sounds of movement towards the door. I hurried as fast and silent as I could to the backroom. I get to the backroom just in time hoping that I wasn't seen. The sound of a single set of footsteps draws closer so I go back to the table and try to slow my breathing.

"Okay, so you said you might have found something." Jacqueline says pulling the curtain to side and entering the room.

"Well maybe, I'm not really sure what I'm looking at." I point to a spot on the old scroll. "see this symbol right here, it appears on a few that I've seen so far. This is the design I saw on the beast's neck. It also matches the one on two guys I happened to run into." I say

"These symbols that you've seen, are you sure that they looked like these?" Jacqueline asks

"Yeah, why do you know what they are?" I ask her

"Well that could prove to be why it's been so difficult finding things. They are for The Black Order of the Dragon." She says

"That doesn't sound like a good thing. What is this dragon thing, some kind of a cult?" I ask

"There's more than one Dragon order so you need to know the difference. The Black Dragon are followers of Ahriman and the Red dragon is Tiamat. They try to recognize both the masculine and feminine demonic ideals of the Vampyric path." Jacqueline explains

"Great that's just what I need is to try to remember subspecies of the fuckers trying to kill me. Is there any up side? You know like not all of them want my head." I say

"Yes and no but I'm going to need some time to find out which group is here and what kind of threat is out there exactly. Why don't you head home for the night and check with me tomorrow." Jacqueline suggests putting her hand on my shoulder.

"Sounds good to me" I say rubbing my tired eyes. The constant reading and searching has worn me down and started to give me a headache. I don't think I've ever stared at stuff I don't understand for so long in my life. That extra caffeine from this morning wore off long ago leaving me hungry, tired and kind of shaky.

"Mind if I take a few of these with me, you know so I can have some light reading before bed?" I say digging through the pile of books I haven't gotten to yet.

Hesitating for a moment, Jacqueline responded in a less than thrilled manner. "Ummm, I guess that would be Okay. Just remember that these are one of a kind and worth a fortune and treat them with respect."

"I get it, no reading them in the crapper or using them as a coaster." I say trying to ease her tension. With the look she shot at me I doubt she is in a joking mood when it comes to these books. As I make my choices of what to take my mind drifts back to the tarp covered pedestal to my right. If she didn't want me looking it has to be pretty special, I mean she's letting take all these and has just met me. While Jacqueline is busy going over the material I found I sneak over and lift the tarp as quickly and quietly as I can.

"HOLY HELL, WHAT IN THE F......."
Jacqueline smacks my hand causing me to drop the tarp and stop mid-word.

"I thought I said to leave stuff alone?" Jacqueline asks giving me look of disapproval

"Sorry, I just had to know what was under there and why it was the only clean thing back here." I say apologetically.

"Well it's not mine and the owner come in once a week to take care of and clean it. As for what it is the short answer is a weapon. Does that answer your question?" she asks as she straights the tarp.

I have more questions now than I did 5 minutes ago but I know when I've over-stepped my bounds. These people are helping me and teaching me and barely know anything about me. I pick up 3 book and stack up the rest for her with my head down. "I promise I didn't mean any disrespect so I'm going to get out of your hair till you call me."

She rest her left hand on my shoulder and raises my chin with her right hand to look me in the eyes and says "Don't beat yourself up about it, just don't let it happen again. Some of the things in here belong to private collectors and are irreplaceable. They trust that I won't let anything happen to them."

Without another word I make my way back to the front of the store with Jacqueline following me. She unlocks the door so I can leave and I walk out. I'm almost to the truck when she says "Hey Jacob".

I turn and look at her still feeling bad about what I did and in a half-hearted voice I say "yeah, what's up?"

She smiles at me and says "It was pretty cool looking wasn't it?"

I set the books on the hood of the truck and hurry back to her "from what I saw, hell yes it was! Was that an ax head on an old sawed off shotgun?"

"Shhh not so loud, and yes but it's much more than that. Ask Sebastian about it when he returns, maybe he will let you hold it." Jacqueline says with a sense of glee.

Once I get the truck started and notice the time. One forty-three, where did the time go. Thinking that I have nothing of any substance to eat at my place I pull into the first place I find. There's not much open at this hour so fast food burgers it is.

I order enough to have something for now and to reheat in the morning now that I have to get those units finished sooner than I wanted. I like my quiet building and now I'm going to have not only more people roaming around, but I'm pretty sure they all want to kill me. I guess it was bound to happen eventually. As I drive home I pull out my phone and check it and see there's still nothing from Jenny. There's a possibility that she was scared off by the shit-storm she ended up in or she finally realized that I'm a freak. Nobody wants to be with a freak that gets stared at wherever they go. War's hell I assume and me being on my own is just a casualty. I crank up the music as I drive to clear my head and forget about the bullshit for a few.

On my way back to the apartment I decide to take a pass by the club we went to the night before to see if there's any late night metal happening. I make a pass by the front of the building and it looks like they were closing up for the night with the crowd heading out the door and inside lights coming on. From the look of the people walking away with the baggy pants and over-sized shirts I'm sure I wouldn't have blend in and fade into the background. These days it would be difficult for me to fit in anywhere with actual lighting if I don't have a hood to cover the scars with.

I make a u-turn three blocks from the club to head to the rear of my building so I can pull the truck right in and not worry about parallel parking this big bastard. Mid-way through the turn I see the truck that Fred was driving earlier following me from about five car lengths back. As I tried to get a look in the window to see who was driving the driver ducked down and gave the truck some gas speeding away.

I pulled the truck into the driveway on the back of my apartment and scooped up my food and books. I wanted to hurry and get inside but I wasn't sure if they had gotten here before me or more were waiting to catch me off guard. I grab an old plastic bag from the floorboard and stick the books inside making them easier to carry. I flipped the seat forward and used my phone for a light as I dug around till my hand finally found what I was searching for, a short handled three pound sledgehammer. I take a few practice swings and grab my bags and move towards the door.

Making my way to the building I move slow and squint my eyes to try and see in the shadows. I make a mental not that I need to replace the outside property lights to make it harder for someone to lurk in the dark.

If I would've known that an ancient asshole and his lackeys would want to drain me or some shit I would have fixed them months ago when they went out. I realized I was lost in thought when I heard the rumbling sound of a truck moving slowly down the street. I ducked into the shadow on the right side of the building near the trash dumpster. As the truck creeped by I peered out of the darkness to see it was not the truck that was following me a few minutes earlier. The driver was a woman trying to apply makeup as she was talking on the phone.

I remained in the shadow for a moment till she passed by to make sure and let my heart rate return to normal. I made my way to the door and opened it as quietly as I could and closed it behind myself. Working my way up the stairs doing my best to not to make a sound which was proving to be harder than it should be with the creaking steps and my inability to not bang the bags against everything in sight. I'm almost to my door when I see there's a note taped to it. Feeling more paranoid now I set the bags down keeping the sledgehammer ready I get to my door and open the note, it reads

"Jacob, the people from earlier got their paperwork turned in so we are going to need to get that unit ready asap. Time is money, and I need that money to keep this place going. Tim"

Well shit, it looks like less research and more work. The worst part about it is the research is for the people that are trying to move in that want keep tabs of me. Maybe it's a good thing that Jenny removed herself from the situation so she wouldn't get hurt. I stuff the note in my right back pocket and walk over and grab my bags no longer caring if someone hears me since the people I'm watching out for are movie in the building soon. I pull out my keys and unlock my door and head inside. Closing the door with my left heel and I stick the sledge under my left armpit and lock the deadbolt and put the chain on and the door brace on the doorknob. Feeling a little safer now, I set the keys and sledgehammer on the table in the hallway as I make my way to the kitchen to reheat my food. I set the bags on the kitchen counter and take two burgers out of the bag and grab a paper plate off the stack by the stove. I unwrap the burgers and put them on the plate and stick it in the microwave. They aren't too cold so I figure one minute should do it. While it heats up I stick the remaining food in the fridge for tomorrow. When the microwave dings I open it and take my plate out and walk over to my chair in the living room grabbing one of the books on my way.

I get comfortable in my chair and start thumbing through the book with my right hand while I hold my burger in my left. I notice that there are notes written in the margins in English so these could be helpful since nothing in this book looks like anything I could figure out on my own. I continue eating and scrolling through the pages reading the notes as I come across them and my eyesight starts to blur. Realizing I'm exhausted I set the book on the floor and finish my food. With the last bite still in my mouth being chewed I stand up and walk to my bedroom to get some sleep and end this day of bullshit.

After staggering down the hall and bumping into everything possible on the way to the bedroom door I'm finally able to kick off these boots off and pass out. I sit on the edge of the bed and pull my left pant leg up and lean over to untie my boot when I feel something move in the bed. I jump up and make a mad dash to the hallway table to grab the sledge. Now with a weapon in hand I sneak back to the room. Reaching around the corner, my hand searches for the light switch. It took a few seconds but I finally find the switch and flip on the light. I gather my courage and run through the bedroom doorway screaming raising the sledgehammer over my head to bring down on whatever is waiting under the covers. I grab covers with my free hand and yank them back and start to swing the hammer down with all of my might.

Jenny sat up quickly and yelled "WHAT THE..."

To prevent from braining Jenny I swing wide and fall off balance landing on my left hip sending the sledge tumbling through the closet door. "Ouch" I say trying to sit up.

"What are you doing here? I've been trying to get hold of you all day." I say rubbing my potential new bruise.

"First off I lost my phone, second I thought I would surprise you and got tired of waiting decided to rest till you got home. And finally what's with the hammer, who do you think you are Thor or something?" Jenny replies still shaken clutching the covers to her chest.

"Hell no I don't think I'm Thor, he's from a different mythology I think. I'm still not sure about all that shit, but I do know that I would never be caught dead in a spandex suit. You freaked me out is all. How did you even get in here? I know I locked up before I left." I say scooting over to the bed with my hand reached out towards Jenny.

She took my hand and I could feel she was shaking and that I scared her. I pulled her to me as I sat on the edge of the bed. She laid her head on my lap and looked up at me.

As she lay there fidgeting with the sheet Jenny said "Some guy named Tim let me in. He was putting the note on your door when I showed up. He said he owned the place and offer to let me in when I said I was your girlfriend."

With a smile I pulled my hands to my chest and said "Wait a minute there, girlfriend? I'm a free spirit and you come in here throwing labels around like you own me".

Jenny sat up quick and hit me in the chest and reared back to swing again when I put my hands up to block the oncoming onslaught. "I'm joking, you're my girlfriend."

She put her hands down and laid her head back in my lap and snuggled up close with her hands wrapped around my leg. "Damn right you better be joking because I own your ass now. After last night I'm not letting you get away. What the hell was that anyway?"

I brushed her hair from off the side of her face and said "I wish I knew but I will ask Mother when I hear from her."

"Hear from her, where did she go? I was actually expecting those two to be here when I came by earlier." she said rolling onto her back to look up at me.

"No clue, she said something about going back to where it all started. She was being all cryptic." I replied

I leaned back on the bed and start to get comfortable. Jenny shifts in the bed till we are laying side by side. I start to twist to put my feet on the bed so I could lay fully on the bed when I realize I'm still wearing my boots. I nudge Jenny slightly so I could get my arm from out from under her and she rolls to her rights side. I sit up and untie my boots and kick them off so they land near the closet door. Not knowing where things stand I leave my shirt and jeans on when I climb under the covers and slide behind Jenny. I wrap my right arm over her lower torso and tuck my left under the pillow. Still unsure if this is Okay with Jenny I try to keep a little space between us. That is until she shifted back against me easing the tension causing both of us faded off to sleep.

I awoke feeling the most rested I've ever felt till I noticed Jenny was not in the bed with me. I got out of bed and kicked around the clothes that were piled up on the floor looking for something more comfortable than the jeans I slept in. I came across a pair of baggy shorts that I usually only wear on laundry day and a faded black t-shirt. Since I was alone I stripped down fast and slipped in my change of clothes wasting no time in case Jenny might walk in. I make my way down the hall when Jenny sticks her head around the corner from the kitchen.

"Morning, or afternoon or whatever it is. Hope you don't mind that I let you sleep so late, you looked like you were enjoying it." Jenny said as she walked to the living room.

Wiping the sleep from my eyes, I stopped to stretch before joining her I said "It's cool, I think that's the first time in a long time I've had a peaceful rest in a while. Now I need coffee."

Jenny points towards the kitchen and says "I ran to the shop down the street and asked some guy named Jessie if you had come in there and what you liked to drink, so I hope it's correct."

I walk into the kitchen and see the cup sitting there on the counter looking so warm and inviting. I pick it up and say, "Well if Jessie made it and knew it was for me than I'm sure it's perfect."

I take a small sip to test the temperature and see it's cooled enough to drink and drink the entire cup down. It was just the way I like it caramel mocha Irish cream with 4 shots of espresso. I head to the fridge to get my leftover burgers from last night and toss them in the microwave. As I open the door to the refrigerator I hear Jenny clear her throat. I look over to see what she wants.

"There's food in the oven staying warm for you." Jenny says muffled from a mouthful of food
"The oven, you mean that thing works?" I say shocked as I open the oven door and pull a plate of food out.

"Yes it works, you are quite possibly the worst maintenance man ever. You know that right?" she says shaking her head.

I walk over to here and sit on the floor with my plate to eat my food next to her and reply with "it's not that I thought it was broke and couldn't fix it, its that I never use the thing. All my food is either ordered in or single serving microwave crap. No reason to go all out making something fancy when it's only been me eating it."

She put her hand on the top of my head and leaned it back so I was looking up at her and said "well that's going to change, you're going to have to do some of the cooking if you plan on keeping me happy."

I smiled and said "Yes dear" then tilted my head back down and continued shoveling food in my mouth

Jenny reached to the floor and picked up the books I had set there last night and started flipping through the top one. "What are these for and how the hell do you know what they say?"

Still eating my food I don't even look up to reply "for the most part I don't have the foggiest of ideas of what they say. I'm more checking the pictures looking for something and if you look there are some translations scribbled in the margins. The what for part is easy, trying to learn what I can about what's after me."

I finish eating and take my plate to the kitchen and sit it in the sink then make my way back to Jenny. She scoots down to sit next to me on the floor so we can look through the books together. Maybe a second set of eyes will come in handy.

Book after book we search the pages for anything that might be useful. Jenny was making notes on a notepad that she found on the end table so we could keep track of where we looked and what could be interesting. I checked the time when I heard a car door slam outside. It was Tim and I haven't done anything to the apartments I needed to work on. I jumped up and meet Tim in the hallway as he was making his way up the stairwell.

"Hey boss, I see that there's going to be a full building before too much longer" I say hoping he doesn't want to see my progress.

"Well that remains to be seen. Somebody still has a lot of work to do." Tim says as he clears the last step and peeks around the corner to look at the destruction that was the unfinished apartment.

"I can only move as fast as the supplies, you know that. I got everything ordered, they were just running low. Something about all the rehab going on around town." I say dodging the blame. If he buys my excuse I can slack off and draw this out a little longer.

"Alright, just get what you can worked on done please. If we can knock out the little crap to the point all we have is the big stuff then it won't take so long to do once the stuff comes in." Tim says with the look of despair knowing this money is the only thing that could get him out of the red.

"Will do. Let me throw on some pants and I will jump right on it." I tell him giving him that little dash of hope he needs to keep afloat.

I head back into my apartment and close the door. Stopping for a moment to rub my head. I can feel the makings of a tension headache building. I head to my room to change my clothes when I hear Jenny heading down the hallway.

I closed the door behind me and rush to grab my work pants. They are an old pair of camouflage pants I got at the thrift store for two dollars so I can afford to mess them up with paint and such. I'm almost changed when there's a knock from Jenny on the door.

"Hey babe, what's up?" Jenny asked leaning against the doorway running her hand on the door.

I button my pants and grab my boots as I walk to the door. I open the door and see her standing there looking worried. "Nothing, I just got to get some work done across the hall in one of the other apartments. There's a few people moving in and he needs them done sooner than later."

"Oh, Okay" she says then flicks me on the nose. "Let me grab my shoes and I'll come with." Jenny skips towards the living room to get her shoes and plopped in the chair need the window. I walk down to join her and put my boots on. After putting her shoes on she picks up the notepad she's been using for the books and says "I can read you some of the stuff I found while you work."

"That sounds good, at least we can spend the day together and maybe the day won't be a complete waste." I tell her as I tie my last boot.

I get up from the chair and look around the room trying to remember where I put my tool belt. Jenny gathered the books and her notes. I grabbed the keys to the apartments I needed to work on and we went across the hall to the first apartment. Once inside I walk to the living room and open the windows and Jenny looks for a good place to sit. She settles on the recliner in the corner of the room.

As I'm opening the second window I hear Jenny clear her throat "Ahem, is this what you were looking for a few minutes ago" I turn and see her holding my tool belt with her right hand.

I walk over to her and take it out of her hand and put it on. Leaning down to kiss her on the forehead and say "Thank you, what would I do without you?"

Sarcastically she says "Starve or die from that crap you eat to start with, but the list goes on"

I adjust my belt, standing there in front of her I reply "Funny, thanks for the vote of confidence. I'll have you know I survived on my own before. I'm not completely useless"

"Hey you asked." Jenny said looking down at the book as she flipped through the pages.

I get my pencil out of my tool belt and pick up a piece of scrap cardboard from the trash pile in the corner of the room. I make my way through the apartment making a list of everything that needs to be done to get the place ready for rent. As I'm walking making notes I yell from the back bedroom "Jenny, if you come across stuff in there just yell."

Jenny yells back from her recliner "Okay, but I don't have the first clue what I'm looking for"

I head back to the living room and say "neither do I, so if you find something in English let me know."

"Oh okay, That's easy enough." Jenny says without looking up from the page. Her eyes skimming from left to right in search of something that stands out.

I decide to tackle the kitchen problems first since there are more small issues on my list in there than anywhere else in this place. I open the cabinet door leading under the sink and see the damp mess waiting for me. Thinking to myself that there's no way I will see where the leak is coming from. I grab a trash bag from the roll on the counter and start filling it from the empty cleaning bottle graveyard that was the cabinet so I could make enough room to get in the space to work.

I finally clear the area I need to work. In the process of doing that I filled the trash bag over half full and set at least a dozen half empty bottles of cleaner on the counter to save for when I need to scrub the filth off later. I put on my headlamp so I can see what I'm doing under here and lay down with my three quarters of my body on the kitchen floor. I hear a chair being drug across the floor. I look up and see Jenny getting situated in a chair near my feet and using the counter for prop up the book she's searching.

Once she's comfortable in her chair sitting cross legged looking like she's studying for a test I say " Did you get lonely out there by yourself?"

"No, just thought I would come keep you company and so I didn't have to yell. There's some weird stuff in these books. Where did you find these things anyway?" jenny asks flipping back and forth in the book.

Blindly digging through my tool belt for my wrench I say "Well yesterday I went to clear my head and see if I could find an occult book store or something that might have something useful about all this bullshit going on. Something that might prove useful and I came across a place down in that artsy district. Turns out the owner knows mother, and she let me take some home to read."

"Go figure, mother would know someone that works at one of those places." Jenny says

"That's kinda what I thought." I say with a chuckle finally finding the pipe wrench. I turn the water line off to be on the safe side and loosen the drain pipe.

Jenny taps my foot with her pencil and says "hey listen to this, I think I found something."

Still working on the drain pipe I say "I'm all ears"

"I found a few notes in the margin that talks about the Black order of the Dragon. It goes on to mention Akhkharu with a line out to the side of it and the words means darkness. Hey that's the name Mother was calling it." Jenny exclaims

I sit up so fast I forget to scoot out from under the sink. This causes me to catch my forehead on the overhang of the cabinet. I fell backwards hitting the back of my head on the loose drain pipe. I push myself out from under the sink slower this time. I sit upright and hold the front and back of my head and say "Did you say that his its name means darkness?"

Jenny tilts the book so I can see for myself and says "yeah, right here. Akhkharu means darkness. They even have it underlined like five times."

Pulling my hands from my head to check for blood and not finding any I take off my headlamp and see I broke it. I toss the lamp towards the trash bag and say "I wonder why mother didn't say anything about that"

Jenny shrugged her shoulders and says "Maybe she didn't know. There's more stuff here, do you want me to keep reading?"

"Yes please, every little bit helps." I say

Running her fingers over the page her hand stops when she finds another passage and reads aloud "Akhkharu has a group of followers that go by Brotherhood of the Darkness. Their numbers are unknown due to their code of secrecy. Many mysteries surround these followers. That's all on this page but I will keep looking"

I clean off my hands with a rag I have on my tool belt and get up off the floor. I walk to the apartment's front door and peek out into the hall to see if anyone is around. I don't see anyone so I close the door and lock it. I walk to the living room window and look down towards the street trying to see Tim's truck, it's not there anymore.

I tell Jenny to come into the living room with the books. I clear off the couch so we can sit there. Sitting side by side I take the notepad from her and read over it trying to find something I remember her writing earlier. "I knew it, that darkness thing is a game changer. Remember this from earlier."

Jenny leans over and reads the lines I have my finger on "To know balance is to experience and master the Darkness. The Gods have created all things from Darkness, for the Darkness is eternal and never-ending"

We look at each other in silence for a moment trying to wrap our heads around what we just found. Stunned from our newly acquired knowledge on what we might be up against we stare lost at the page. It took a few minutes to regain composure and get back to reading but we both knew it needed done.

In one of the books I came across scribblings that mentioned the Black Order. It went into detail of the order being of two parts, the black dragon Ahriman and the Red dragon Tiamat. It said that some believe that this was written to explain a war by different areas in the ancient royal families. It described that the royals wanted to take the power back from the Gods with a select group of people that processed different magic. There were no translations after that part.

It looked like things were scratched out or erased. Almost like someone didn't want others to know what it said. I pointed this out to Jenny and she suggested that we set it aside for when Mother returned to see if she can translate. I agree with Jenny and toss the book to my left on open area of the couch.

Jenny continues scavenging through the foreign text and confusing art work to find more on the this Darkness or Brotherhood and I went back to work on the sink. After getting everything disassembled I find the problem and tell Jenny I need to run to the store area downstairs to see if I have any o-rings laying around and head out the door. While in the storeroom my phone rings and it's Jacqueline. I answer with questions ready "Hey, just one of the people I need to talk to. I have questions and I think you have answers"

"I bet you do but over the phone is not the way to do it, can you come to the bookstore?" Jacqueline asked. Her voice was quiet and seemed rushed. Almost like there was something wrong and she was trying to not let anyone hear.

"Yeah, I'll be there in about....." I began to say when she cut me off

"No times, no more information. Just get here" Jacqueline said as the phone line went dead
I rushed upstairs to my apartment to get the truck keys off of the table and before walking too far I turned and went back for the sledgehammer. I put the sledge in the loop on my tool belt as I headed across the hall to get Jenny so she could go with me.

"Hey babe, we have to go, grab the books and hurry please." I tell jenny waving my arms to indicate that she needs to hurry.

"Where, what's going on?" she asks grabbing her stuff off of the couch and jogging towards the door with a worrisome look.

"I'll explain on the way. We need to hurry so do you want to take the truck or your car?" I say locking up both apartments.

"Mine's faster and easier to get through traffic" Jenny says pulling her keys out of her pocket. "you know where we're going so you drive."

I follow Jenny down the front staircase to her car. I unlock the passenger side door letting her inside and head around to the driver's side while I look up and down the street for any vehicles or people that could be watching or waiting. I get in the driver's seat and fire up the beast.

I've heard the car rumble when it starts before but not ever noticed the vibrations and power that the car possessed until now. I rev the engine a few times and shift it into gear. Tires squeal as I accelerate and we were on our way.

Feeling I should explain what's happening and why we had to leave so fast I look over at Jenny. The look of concern is evident on her beautiful face. I say "You remember me telling you where I got those books and how the lady knows Mother?"

A little hesitant she answers "Yeah, what does that have to do with anything? Did something happen?"

Still watching the road I continue explaining "Well her name is Jacqueline, and she called while I was looking for parts. I'm not sure what is going on but she said I needed to get there fast and hung up"

"Okay, but she just met you. There had to be someone else she could call if there was a problem." Jenny says.

I reach over and put my hand on her thigh and squeeze lightly and say "Maybe she found something important and couldn't say it in front of people. It is a store and all. There might be customers that wouldn't understand what she's talking about and get freaked out."

Jenny nods her head and seems more upbeat and says "Yeah that's probably it. So you could probably slow down to only going twice the speed limit."

I look down at the speedometer and see I'm going almost eighty miles an hour through town. "Shit, sorry. I'm use to the truck." I let off the gas pedal and slow down to thirty-five just in time for a cop to turn the corner in front of me. I take a left on the next block and follow that for a few blocks until we see the bookstore just ahead on the right. I park the car about half a block away and we sit for a moment watching the storefront for activity.

There were no cars in front of the store and nobody has come in or out when I see Jacqueline open the door and look up and down the street frantically. I step out of the drivers side door and wave so she can see its me. She gives me a slight nod of acknowledgment and the faintest of waves to come inside. I lean down to look into the car and motion for Jenny to get out and follow me inside. Jenny and I move towards the store in a fast walk to not draw any unwanted attention to ourselves in case the place is being watched.

As we approach the door Jacqueline is ready for us with an open door. I take Jenny's hand and pull her close behind me. I wanted to enter first since I didn't know what we were walking into.

Crossing the threshold Jacqueline swings the door closed and locks it. We got no further than another step when sparks and what resembled lightning came shooting off of Jenny. She dropped the books and notepad she had in her left hand and still had a grip of my hand with her right.

I look at Jacqueline as I'm being electrocuted and yell out "WHAT'S HAPPENING TO HER?"

Jacqueline is shielding her eyes and trying to avoid the electric bolts coming off Jenny and responds back with fear in her voice "SHE'S GIFTED, LIKE YOU! GIVE HER YOUR MEDALLION QUICKLY!"

The electricity that was pulsing through my body had dropped me to my knees. I force my muscles on my free arm to work and with every ounce of strength I reach to my neck and grab for the string holding the medallion and force it over my head. I see the horror and pain in Jenny's eyes as she is riding the lightning storm from hell. I had to do this, I had to get this around her neck to stop what is happening. I grab the counter and push myself to the standing position. Still holding Jenny's hand I pull her towards me as I work my way forward. With one final burst of strength I reach and drape the string over her head. As quickly as it started it was over. Jenny collapsed into my arms causing both of us to drop to the floor.

As the smoke rises from our bodies I look up to see Jacqueline staring with her hand over her mouth in utter shock. She takes her hand from her mouth and says in a shaky voice "Why didn't you say she was gifted?"

Looking up in confusion still holding Jenny tight I say "I didn't know, she never told me"

Still confused Jacqueline says "Does she even know, or does she know what you are?"

I cradle Jenny's head and softly say "Yes, yes she does and it didn't bother her. Mother explained everything to her. She's the girl that I told you about. You know the one I saved from Akhkharu."

Leaning down to help me get Jenny upright Jacqueline says "That explains something I was wondering about. Let get her to the back so she can rest while you tell me what you know about her."

Once standing I scoop Jenny up in my arms and follow Jacqueline through the maze of shelves to the back of the store. Jacqueline holds the curtains open so I can get through and I notice that the room looks worse than before. Stepping over boxes and books that lay open on the floor I make my way to a padded leather chair on the north wall.

Jacqueline meets me by the chair and brushes the dust from where Jenny's head will come to rest. I gently set her in the chair and slide one of the boxes across the floor for Jenny to use as a footrest. Taking off my hoodie I ball it up and place it under Jenny's head. With the smoke subsiding from my body and clothes I take Jacqueline's arm and pull her towards the doorway.

Now feeling we are far enough away from Jenny to talk without her hearing what we are saying and freak her out more when she wakes up I quietly say "What was that? When I came in the first time I just felt like I had some bad Thai food and she comes in and turns into a walking talking Tesla coil"

Jacqueline with a bewildered look on her face places one hand on my chest and says "I've never seen anything like that happen before. Honestly I know the Rowan tree barrier has different effects on the gifted but I've only heard of one incident where electricity flew from the body and they exploded in seconds."

Feeling furious I push her hand from my chest and say "You better be damn glad that didn't happen"

Trying to calm myself and regain composure I take a few deep breaths and pace the floor for a moment and then return in front of Jacqueline to ask "who was this one other person and why did they, you know go boom?"

Jacqueline thinks for a moment and replies "From what the story says, they were a great magician with control over time and space. I think the reason Jenny survived is because you grounded her and took some of the effects onto yourself. Was there any indication that she had a gift."

Lost in my thoughts and trying to think back of the times we had spent together I tell Jacqueline "No, nothing that stands out," then like a flash it hits me "When I went into her mind this first time and woke up I found out it hadn't happened yet and was actually days before it was going to happen,"

Jacqueline stood shaking her head listening intently. Feeling stupid that I had forgotten about something so important I told her about our first big kiss when time felt like it froze and everything went silent.

We have only known each other for a short time but I've seen very few accept me for who I am and before Jenny there was no one that wasn't part of this gifted world. I pace the floor waiting for Jenny to come to. She has moved a little but nothing that showed she was waking up anytime soon.

I was getting fidgety and had to do something, anything to make time pass when I remembered that Jacqueline called me here for something. I looked around for Jacqueline and didn't see her but I saw the destruction and needed to know if this was because of me.

I pull back the curtain to head to the main store front and almost run into Jacqueline. She was making her way to the backroom with a tray carrying three cups and a pot of what appears to be some kind of tea of the weakest coffee ever made.

I reach out to take the tray from her and Jacqueline says "I got this, you just hold the curtain. I thought you would like something to calm your nerves."

I hold the curtain back till she's into the room and then move towards the table to clear a spot for her to set it down. She stands patiently as I make room on the table. My movements are frantic and clumsy and can't seem to calm down which causes me to trip on the clutter more than once. I decide to look for a few chairs for us to sit mainly so I don't keep falling over everything possible. I make it back with two chairs and set mine down so I can keep an eye on Jenny. I want to be there as she returns to the land of the living.

When we are seated Jacqueline fills and hands me a cup. I take it and put it to my lips taking a small sip and ask "This is good, what is it?"

She chuckles softly and says "It's nothing magical or mystical just good ole chamomile tea with lavender"

Afraid I gave the wrong impression I tell her "Sorry, I didn't mean it like that. My brain is just all over the place."

Jacqueline puts her hand on my wrist and says "I know it is child, it's okay. Try to relax some, I'm sure she will be fine."

Leaning forward in my chair with my elbows on my knees I say "I just want to know why I'm up and energized while she is out cold. Can you explain that to me?

She looks puzzled for a minute and says "I think it's because you two are connected in some way stronger than other like you. There are tales of the original families trying to cross the gifts with other royals to get a more powerful offspring.

What they didn't realize until later was that certain gifts compliment others and a bond forms between them that is unbreakable. What I think happened is that the tie between you two was stronger than the wards that were in place and the Rowan tree. She in essence is your other half."

As what she told me sank in I sat back in the chair silent. What she said opened everything up for questions that I had to ask but I was having trouble forming words or even sounds. Knowing there was no way to know if what she was saying was fact or just fairy tales I decided to push it to the back burner for a short time to let it process.

I pick up my cup of tea thinking it should be cooled down enough to drink and say "You called me here for something, what's going on that I needed to rush over?"

As she leaned forward a little and set her cup down Jacqueline said "Oh yes, that. Well I got a text from Mother with just numbers and letters. It's an old code we come up with to keep people guessing if the messages ever fell into the wrong hands."

Curious I ask "What was the message, is she in trouble? Was it for me?"

Jacqueline could see the suspense was too much for me and spoke calmly "It WAS for you but it was something I have to show you rather than tell you."

Jacqueline stands up and signals me to follow her and whispers "The bastards that tore the place up thought they searched everywhere but they didn't." She stands next to the solid floor to ceiling wooden bookcase and runs her left hand down the side and presses gently till I hear a click. Then with her right hand grips the third shelf and shifts it slightly forward till another click happens. At that moment the sound of gears grinding and weights dropping into place filled the room. The what would seem immovable bookcase glided open revealing another room. Everything in here was pristine and neatly put up. I spot the case holding the shotgun-ax thing that I so wanted to play with. In all the confusion I didn't even notice that it wasn't in the other room.

In total awe as I look around the hidden room I say "What is all this stuff and why is it hidden in here."

She looks at me and says "You must never speak of this room to anyone, there are only four people that know it even exists." I nod my acknowledgment.

She continues. "This is for things that aren't supposed to have survived through the years or are only believed as myth. Now the reason I'm showing you this is, Mother asked me to give you something."

She moves forward in the room and I without thinking walk right behind here into the vault. Jacqueline says without turning to look at me as she is focused on where she is going "this room has stronger wards than the main entrance so whatever you do don't cross the threshold. It takes a specific medallion."

I tap her on the right shoulder and say with a wide eyed worried look "What happens if I didn't hear that part in time and walked in here anyway?"

She stares at me with complete shock and says "That can't be, you shouldn't have been able to pass the threshold."

Now even more freaked out I say "Am I going to explode or something?"

She claps her hands together not really knowing what to think and says "If you haven't died by now I'm assume you are safe and they wards had no effect. Just to be on the safe side just wait here and I will fetch what I need."

Not wanting to move and cause any more harm I stay put. "You know you aren't the most reassuring person don't you?" I say to Jacqueline. She didn't respond to my comment instead she removed a key from her pocket went to the case holding the shotgun-ax. Leaning over to look underneath to find a key hole she inserted the key and a hidden drawer popped open from the front of the case. She slide the drawer open the rest of the way and removed an odd looking book. The cover resembled leather of some sort. As Jacqueline came closer to me I could see that the book was crudely made. The leather was black and had hair still attached. It was a patchwork of pieces stitched together by what looked like strands of hair woven together to make braids. She handed me the book and once in my hands it had a familiar feel, like something I've recently encountered but couldn't put my finger on till it came to me, it was the newly exposed flesh from where Akhkharu had cut me.

Bewildered I look up at Jacqueline. My hands still caressing the book in disbelief I ask in a shaky and uncertain voice "Is this... is this made from what I think it is?"

Jacqueline confused with my question responds with a question of her own "what do you think it is?"
My anxiety getting the better of me, I shout "FLESH, HUMAN FLESH!" I cover my mouth as surprised as she was that I yelled at her.

She takes the book from my hands slowly and sets it down on the small table behind her and turns to me in a calming tone says "It is flesh, but it's not exactly human. It's been said it's from one of the old gods. Why would you think that it's human?"

I turn to check if Jenny is still unconscious in the chair and look back at Jacqueline and say "Because of this." I untuck my shirt and pull it off over my head and the moment Jacqueline sees my exposed black flesh that was left from my encounter with Akhkharu she gasps. With wide eyes and shock she stares at the blackness between the gashes left by the claw marks. Jacqueline picks up the book of flesh with her right hand and takes a step closer to me.

She leans in holding the book close to her chest, reaches with her left hand to touch my black flesh. The moment before Jacqueline touches me she looks up to see if it's okay with me. I nod yes and she turns her attention back to my exposed scar. Her mouth still gaping in disbelief as she has never encountered anyone or anything else like this before.

After several moments of examination Jacqueline takes a step back and lowers her head to regain her composure. I take that time to put my shirt back on and peek out of the room at Jenny. Jacqueline puts her hand on my shoulder to turn me around. Struggling to make sense of what she was just shown she says "Mother never told me about this, do you know what it is or why? How long has it been visible?"

I look at her as confused as the first time I saw it and say "Wait, are you saying Mother knows what this is, because she told me she didn't know and had to check around. It hasn't been there long, it showed up when we cleaned the wound that I got from that first time hitchhiking in Jenny that turned out hadn't happened yet. I'm sorry I'm rambling, I'm just as lost as you about it."

We walk back out of the hidden room to the storeroom and Jacqueline closes the entrance. As she is locking everything back up I head over to check on Jenny. I can see Jenny has shifted in her chair a little and was making a barely audible groan. I rush over to see if she's coming to and place my left hand on her cheek to let her know I'm there. She shifts in her chair and a labored smile comes to her lips. Jenny opens her eyes and blinks a few times and was out again. I feel a little relief and the thought that she is coming around even if it is very slowly.

I look to the left and right to see where Jacqueline was to see if she noticed what Jenny had done and see her sitting at the table. I walk over and sit down near her hoping she can give me more insight into what the hell is happening to me and why it bothers her so much. Without warning Jacqueline begins firing questions at me "Do you know your parents well? Did they raise you? Where were you born? How long have you known you had a gift?"

I hold up my hand to stop her hurried interrogation and say "Okay first thing first, you can ask me anything and I will tell you what I know but please one question at a time." She shakes her head in acknowledgment and I say "well the parents thing is a bit confusing. They were raising me in a hippy commune, this till the place got raided and I was taken into state custody. With all the scars they assumed I was being beaten or some shit. I really don't remember much from when I was younger anyhow. The dreams and scars started after I fell and cracked my head open. Things were kinda fuzzy for a while but I'm just going off of what I was told. As for where was I born, that's a mystery to me as well. Since the state and hospitals pretty much raised me and had no records of my birth they just gave me a generic one that they filled in the blacks themselves."

Jacqueline stared at me like I just spoke complete gibberish. I could see her trying to compose more questions from the bomb of worthless information I unloaded. Finally she said "So really don't know anything about where you came from or what you are, do you?"

Surprised by her question I ask "What do you mean what I am? I thought I was just one of those hitchhiker things."

She smiled at my use of the term hitchhiker and said "No child, you are much more than a mere hitchhiker as you called it. If I'm correct, and I believe I am than that would explain why Mother wanted you to have this book."

Not knowing what to think of finding out I'm something completely different than what I've been told I am I ask the first thing that comes to mind. "So what's so special about this book other than it's made from someone like me?"

Jacqueline scooted forward in her chair to be closer to the table and slid to book over to me and said "Open it and I will show you what's so special.

I slide the book closer and open the cover to the first page. The pages are made from the same black flesh as the cover. At first glance the pages seemed blank and I said "Okay now what there's nothing here but more freaky skin?" Jacqueline pointed at the page where my hand rested and as I looked for myself symbols began to appear. The symbols were had a red glow and only came into view where my hand touched. The images were completely foreign at when I looked but as I watched them come and go they made sense and I could understand what was there.

I looked up at Jacqueline and said "What does this mean, I can't read it but I know what it says. It's like a voice in my head reading to me."

Amazed as I was, she said "It can only mean one thing, you are what I thought you were. You are a half breed or a demigod so to speak. That book has remained closed for centuries. It was made by the gods and can only be opened and read by one of their own."

I jumped to my feet, knocking my chair backwards and shoved the book away from me and said in a horrified tone "What in the holiest of Hells, am I a bastard of some demon god thing?" my raised voice causes Jenny to stir. Frozen in place, not knowing if I should check on her or wait for an answer I waited.

Jacqueline reached for me from her chair to come closer and sit. I figured it was for the best because I wasn't quite sure how much longer my legs were going to function. This revelation hit me harder than anything I have ever felt before. The fact that Jacqueline and mother might have known makes me question who can be trusted. Until a short time ago I didn't even know Jenny was gifted but remembering what Mother had said about 5 nearby but only 4 know leaves my mind reeling. I feel around for my chair and notice I had gone further back than I had thought. I drag the chair closer to the table and sit. I lean forward resting my elbows on the table with my head hung and asked Jacqueline "How much of this did or does Mother know?"

In a comforting voice Jacqueline says "There's a lot about Mother that's a mystery. She doesn't share a lot of personal information with people, gifted or otherwise." I could see the discomfort in her face and hear the nerves in her voice. Something was scaring her and I'm not sure if it was me or talking about Mother like this but she continued. "How long have you been in the area and where were you before you came to the city?"

Confused by her line of questioning I look up at her and say "I don't know, I got out of the state hospital at 18 and I'm 29 now soooo eleven years. Before here the state bounced me around a lot so no place in particular for very long. Why do you ask?"

Jacqueline leans forward placing he hand on her chin and thinks for a second and says "That's around the same time as when Mother and Sebastian came to town as well."

I shake my head and say "That doesn't mean anything, I've only known her for a year and a half maybe two tops."

Jacqueline shrugs and says "Maybe it's just one big coincidence. That's more of a question for her to answer."

Rubbing my temples with my fingertips, I say "This is too much to process right now. There's questions on top of questions and no answers till Mother decides to grace us with her presence. I need a break."

At that moment Jenny shifted in her chair and gave a loud groan. Her eyelids slowly opened as she shifted to sit upright. Jenny was struggling so I hurried over to her side placing a hand on her shoulder to guide her and make sure she didn't fall forward onto the ground. With Jenny on my mind, nothing else mattered. These things can wait.

When Jenny was up and moving Jacqueline tried to explain what happened to her but Jenny was having a hard time grasping what was being said. I decide it was time to leave and take her back to my place. At least there I can get away from here and collect my thoughts while I keep an eye one Jenny. We say our goodbyes and I help Jenny to the car.

On the drive back one thought lingered, this is all my fault. I drove carefully but with a purpose, watching around every turn and constantly checking the mirrors for anyone following. I was doing my damnedest to avoid talking or looking at Jenny. If it all works in my favor she won't ask me anything until later. My thoughts are frantic but they are all circling the fact that without me around none of this would've happened. Akhkharu wouldn't be here looking for me, Jenny wouldn't have been targeted, Jacqueline wouldn't have had her store trashed and people in KC would be safe. I must have been in a zone deep in thought because I never noticed Jenny's hand resting on top of mine while I held the shifter until she squeezed it.

I quickly look her way and see her give me a faint smile and she said "But, then I wouldn't have you."

Confused on what she was saying I almost missed the turn. I hit the brakes and cut the wheel nearly missing an old Volvo station wagon. Paying closer attention this time I turn down the radio and ask "What's that, what do you mean I wouldn't have you?"

Jenny sat upright and looked at me while squeezing my hand again said "It's not your fault and if you weren't here now I wouldn't have you in my life."

Floored by the words she is saying I feel like I'm losing my mind. Could I have had my entire internal conversation out loud and if so how much did I actually say. Then without a word spoken I hear Jenny's voice in my head say "I'm not sure how but I can hear your thoughts, can you hear mine?"

I hit the brakes and slam the car into park. Turning my body to face her and there must have been pure horror on my face because the was Jenny looked at me was as if I scared her. Out loud is ask "How did you do that? I could hear you in my head."

Jenny placed her hand on my leg and softly said "We can talk about this when we get back to the apartment, Okay. We don't need to try to figure this out in the middle of the road."

It must have been the stress of the day getting to me or the tea from earlier but a wave of exhaustion came over me causing me to yawn. I shifted back properly in my seat and shifted the car and we continued to my apartment. Not a single word was said or a touch shared for the remainder of the drive.

I find a parking spot a little less than a half a block from the front of my building and park. The silence between jenny and I was deafening. I was trying to control my thoughts and not to show fear but that was all I could think about. We didn't touch during the walk to the front of the building. As she took the first step into the building I grabbed her hand and turned her towards me and said "I'm sorry, you must think I'm the biggest fucking idiot of all time."

Jenny's mood changed from a gloomy depression to a cheerful smile and said "Well, not of all time but you are up there."

I pull her to me and hug her tightly and kiss her. Her voice pops in my head again and says "Hearing your voice while I was out is what brought me back."

I step back still holding her and say "Okay, enough of that until we get up stairs and we can figure out what's going on."

"Fine" Jenny says with pouting lips playfully.

After we get up to my apartment and kick off our shoes in the hallway I head into the bedroom to change while Jenny went to the living room. I had just removed my shirt when I heard a thud of something heavy hitting the floor coming from the living room. Fear struck me like a hammer on an anvil. It seemed that I couldn't run towards the sound fast enough. Running down the hallway I couldn't see Jenny. I scanned the room frantically looking for her, then I heard her.

Jenny had dropped to her knees near the window. She was sobbing uncontrollably, face in her hands. I came up behind her and sat down, wrapping my arms around her pulling her to me to comfort her. She melted into me with her limbs going limp. The only movement from Jenny was the jerking, heaving motion as she wept.

Between the sobs came her voice in my mind "Why is this happening to me? What did I do to deserve this, whatever this is?"

All I could do was rock her in my arms and whisper "I don't know, but we will figure it out". The thought lingering inside that everything that is happening to her is because of me.

Jenny sits up and pushes me back slightly to look me in the eyes and says "Stop it, just stop blaming yourself. There was evil in this world long before you came along."

Leaning back on my left arm still half holding her with my right arm on her waist I say "I know that but if I wouldn't have fallen all those years ago…. I don't know maybe I could've just gone through life oblivious to all this hocus-pocus bullshit."

Jenny gave me an angry glare crossing her arms and says "so you would have been happy to have never met me, to not know the other things that go on in the world, and just wined up as another nameless victim."

I drop my head for a moment, knowing what I said hurt her and that was never my intention. I say "I'm sorry, I didn't mean it like that. Meeting you and being with you is the best thing I could ever ask for. I'm just saying that maybe if I were normal then maybe none of this would've happened and you and I could have had a normal life."

She relaxes a little leaning into me and resting her head on my chest and say "Oh you think you could get with me if you were normal. Please, it took an ancient god or something attacking in dreams for you to finally talk to me and you still stumbled over your words."

I hold her a little tighter and say "Oh come on, you have to give me some credit here. That was all part of my plan. It worked didn't it."

She looked up slightly kissing my cheek and say "I guess it did. I could've done without being electrocuted at a bookstore, that shit hurt."

"I know, remember I was being shocked too. According to Jacqueline you're lucky, she said something about the last person that got shocked exploded."

Jenny sat up fast and started smacking me with every word saying "Why would tell me that?"

Reeling back and blocking the flurry of slaps I say "Stop hitting me for a sec." Jenny stopped swinging and waited for me to finish. "From what she said, since you and I were holding onto each other I absorbed some of the juice and that we are connected or something. I think Jacqueline should be the one to explain that because I'm as lost as you are."

I put my hands down when I assumed I was safe. Jenny leaned back into me and started to relax again. I felt I better tell her the last bit of information before she sees it in my head so I say "Oh yeah, I found out something else kinda important while you were out cold."

Relaxed leaning back into me she starts running her fingers down my arm and says "Oh really, what's that?"

I hesitate for the briefest of moments and brace myself and finally utter the words I was afraid to say out-loud "That I'm half god"

Jenny must be completely mentally exhausted because her response wasn't what I was expecting when she said "That figures. Let's go to bed" I agreed with her and we went to the bedroom.

That night I dreamed of an ancient time where beast and gods walked the earth and ruled from massive temples. People giving offerings of food, gold, jewelry and some offering their own daughters. I watched all of this from a tower window. One of the royal families was delivering a young girl in golden chains. Her face was covered as she was led to the alter. A god sat on a throne had skin of black much like the book and my own. The God signaled for the veil to be removed and when it was pulled back the girl looked exactly like Jenny. The God looked at the girl then up at my window. This caused the girl to look my way as well. When our eyes connected she appeared to recognize me. That was when I woke up in a cold sweat.

As I sat up in bed I did my best not to disturb Jenny. I slowly turned to my right and put my feet on the floor and placed my elbows on my knees leaning forward. I need to figure out what it means. It was so vivid, I have to write this down so details won't get forgotten and lost forever. As I look around the room trying to think of where paper and a pen might be I feel Jenny roll over my direction and place her hand on my back.

In a half awake yawning voice Jenny says "You will never believe the dream I had. It's weird because I hardly ever dream much less remember it, but it felt so real."

I turn back to her and say "Me too. I saw some weird shit in mine."

Jenny snuggles up to me and says "Well at least you weren't chained up and sold to some creepy looking guy with pitch black skin."

It took me a moment to realize what she just said and then it hit me "Wait, what? Say that again!"

Jenny still lying close with her eyes closed says "You heard me, you aren't the only one allowed to dream of weird shit."

Now wide awake I shift to look at her and ask "Were there big golden temples and did you see some sort of tower on your right?"

Jenny confused by my question propped herself up on her right arm and cleans the sleep from her eyes and says "Yeah, there was another one of those black skinned creatures in the window. Why do you ask, was that in one of those books we've been reading or something?"

Looking her straight in the eyes I say "I had the same dream, well sort of. I was the thing in the tower looking down. The girl in chains looked like you but I wasn't sure until you told me about your dream."

Jenny reaches across my lap for the night stand. She opens the drawer and grabs a pen and note pad out. Handing me the pad and pen she says "Here take this and write down everything you can remember of your dream and I'll go in the living room and do the same. When we're down we will compare notes. Agreed?"

Giving her my nod of agreement, I see she is waiting for a more verbal response. Not wanting to drag things out and forget things, I say "Agreed."

Jenny gets out of bed and heads out the door and heads to the living room. I began writing and everything rushes back to me just as vivid it was in my dream. A little over an hour passes and I think I finally finished with every tiny detail that I remembered. I gather my notes and get up and walk to the living room and see Jenny set her pen down.

I ask "Are you all done?"
She nods and reaches out to me trying to grab the note pad and says "Yep, gimme, I want to see what your says."

I gladly pass my notes to her and take hers off the coffee table to see what she had written. Knowing this was from her perspective I felt like I was being a little invasive reading it. That feeling went away when a few thing started to match up. There were words that she wrote on here that I remembered hearing but I have no idea what they mean. I have a feeling there will be more questions than answers, which means more research in the future.

I have my pen out and ready as I read Jenny's notes. As I come to something that I remember or a word that isn't English I circle it for later. I look up and see Jenny had the same idea. Soon it went from the random word or line being circled to entire paragraphs and then pages. Towards the end everything she wrote was the way I saw it but from her angle and not from my bird's eye view.

When we were both finished reviewing what each other had written we sat next to one another and compared the similarities, and there were a lot of them. Looking from page to page to ensure we didn't miss anything that might come into question later we worked in tandem. Our thoughts and motions were in sync as if two halves of a whole. Things continued for another half hour until the sound of squeaking brakes of a big truck caught our attention.

I got up and went to the window to see what was going on outside. Looking down I see a black box truck parked in front of the building. There wasn't anyone standing by the truck. Jenny walked over and rested her chin on my left shoulder and asked "What's going on down there?"

Squinting to see in the truck's window I reply with "I'm not sure but I doubt it's anything good, here take a look."

Jenny squeezed in next to me to try and see what's happening and says "Hey I know that truck, that's Fred's. He uses it for when they go to out-of-town shows. Karl's posted pictures of them in that truck many times."

Still trying to see I ask "What do you mean by posted?"
Jenny takes a step back and crosses her arms and says "You've got to be joking, posted as in on his MyWorld account."

I turn my head to see her standing there giving me a glare like I'm crazy person and I ask "Don't look at me like that, you know I kept to myself before you came along." I stand up and turn with my hands up in an I surrender motion and say "Yes I am a caveman and I know nothing of your new fangled thing, teach me oh wise one."

Jenny punched me in the ribs lightly and says "You're damn right I'm the wise one and you better remember that."

I put my hands down and pull Jenny in close to hold her as we look out the window. Jenny turns with her back to me leaning against me and says "Well MyWorld is a social media service that only about a billion people use to post pictures, videos and other meaningless crap just so you can have perfect strangers to give you approval for your stupid actions."

I hold her and slightly rock back and forth and say "Oh okay, so I'm not missing anything"

Jenny says "Not really"
A few minutes pass and we are still watching out the window with no new developments, almost as if they knew we were watching. As jenny and I turn to go back to the couch we notice the passenger side door open, out stepping chatty Cathy from the bar. He walks to the back of the truck where he's met by Fred. Fred unlocks and rolls open the back door.
Jenny asks "What do are doing?"

Not really able to see inside the back of the box truck I reply with "I'm not 100% sure but my guess is moving in."

Jenny walks back to the couch and plops down saying "Most people would prefer to wait till the place is ready" and then returns to the notes.

Stepping away from the window I walk over and sit on the arm of the couch. I rub Jenny's shoulder and say "How about this for an idea? We get ready, go eat some food and see what Jacqueline thinks about all this."

Jenny looks up at me questioning my logic "Is she going to electrocute me till I pass out again?"

I get up to head to the bedroom to get ready and without looking back I say "I doubt it, pretty sure that's a welcome to my store for the first time thing."

As I'm walking and taking off my shirt I get nailed in the back of the head with a pillow from the couch. I continued my way down the hall and said "I guess I can call ahead and let her know to see if it's cool first, but I'm assuming the charm you're wearing will make your entry less shocking"

"Not funny jackass" Jenny hollers from the other room.

We both got ready and headed the back of the building to avoid any unwanted attention from Fred and his friend. The weather wasn't bad out today and Jenny wanted to get some fresh air, so we walked. The diner wasn't too far off and living where I did had its advantages with everything being pretty close. Normally I would be more covered up but I guess being around her this short time has made me not care as much about it. She grabbed my hand and down the road we went.

While we ate I text Jacqueline to let her know we were going to stop by to show her something and get her take on it. She responded with saying "good, some things have changed that you need to know." We finished up eating and slowly walked the six blocks to the shop so our food could settle. There's nothing worse than trying to fight right after eating. It's almost as bad as trying to run in flip-flops.

As we the store came in sight both Jenny and I looked up and down the street for any signs of danger or anything out of place. The area was pretty dead except for a few hipsters walking their dander-free, hypoallergenic, vegan, super breed dogs that looked miserable. I couldn't help but think one day those dogs are going to snap and gnaw off their faces. The coast appearing clear we finish our trek to the front door. I pull on the handle only to find it locked. I wipe off a spot on the window to see if I can spot anyone or anything moving around inside. The stores lights were off and I couldn't make out any definite images so I guess I have to revert to plan C. I take out my phone and start to text Jacqueline and Jenny put her hand on mine to stop me.

Jenny looks at the store front and then to me and says "With everything going on how do we know that was her that responded to the text earlier? Maybe you should call so you can know for sure."

I delete my text and hit the call button and say "That's not a bad idea, I knew there was a reason to keep you around. You're the brains, I'm the brawn or whatever."

Jenny looked me up and down and chuckled "Yeah, brawn. If you say so"

I look through the window while the phone rang and said under my breath "you weren't complaining when I saved your ass."

Jenny snapped back with "What did you say?"

I turn toward her and mouth the words "Can't you see I'm on the phone"

Finally the phone is answered by Jacqueline "What's taking you so long?"

"Well we are outside and the door is locked" I say

In an apologetic voice Jacqueline says "I'm sorry, I meant to tell you to come to the back door."

Surprised I say "There's a back door, why am I just hearing about this?"

"Of course there's a back door, it's part of city code. You know for fires and stuff. Just take the alley to the left and I will let you in."

I hang up the phone and look at Jenny and say "Apparently there's a back door, she's going to meet us there to let us in."

Jenny follows me around the left side of the building. We move slowly watching around corners and beside the dumpster. Once we get to the back of the store we see the heavy steel door and I bang on it to let Jacqueline know we are there. The door opens and in the dim light I see a figure much larger than what I was expecting, Sebastian.

Happy and surprised I say "You're back"

Sebastian waved us to come in "Mother's waiting"

I let Jenny go first since we know it's safe and I follow patting Sebastian on the arm as I walk by and say "We always have the best talks"

Sebastian slams the door and locks it. We follow him through the hallway to where Mother and Jacqueline are waiting for us. As we walk into the room I see the two women sitting at the table talking quietly as they look over several of the books and scrolls that were there.

Walking up to the table I look for a few extra chairs and say "I'm so glad you're back, there's so much to tell you. Soooo what did you do on your vacation?"

Mother gave me a dirty look over the top of the reading glasses perched on the end of her nose. She motioned for me to hurry up and sit. I pulled up two chairs to the table and started to grab a third and Sebastian shook his head no and I set it down. I sat to the left of Mother and Jenny sat next to me.

Sliding her glasses up on her nose with her left index finger she said "It was hardly a vacation child. What's that you got there, research?" motioning for the notebooks I set down before getting the chairs.

I pick them up and hand them to mother. As she starts reading I say "It's not exactly research, it's a dream that Jenny and I had last night, separately. Sort of, I don't know what it means. That's kinda why we're here."

Mother finishes reading the pages and passes them to Jacqueline to have her read them. Mother leans forward to rest her elbows on the table and looks at Jenny and asks "Jenny darling, what can you tell me of your family?"

Jenny shrugs slightly seeming slightly uncomfortable by the question and replies with "Not much, I've been own since I was 16. I was an orphan and in foster care before that. I don't really know anything about my family history if that's what you're asking."

Mother leaned back in her seat with a little grin. Her reaction confused not only Jenny but me as well. It caused Jenny to pull her legs up in her chair to sit with her knees to her chest and arms wrapped Around her chin. I reached over to her and placed my hand on her arm to comfort and try to help her relax. I've never asked or even thought of what her family situation was. I figured she would tell me when she was ready. My background isn't the best, so I understand not sharing.

Looking over at Mother I ask "What made you ask that question, was it something in the notes?"

"Something like that. You see with a gift like yours, it's tricky. See you haven't really pushed yourself to the full potential of the ability." Mother says

"What do you mean, full potential? What else is there that I can do other than sit back and watch bad shit happen to others. Other than the one time I saw something that hadn't happened yet."

Mothers' grin turns to a full smile and she reaches out and places her hand on my arm and says "Oh child, there are so many things I want teach you if you are ready to learn."

A little excited with the possibilities that could happen from learning and knowing what waits I sit straight up in my seat and say "I'm ready, when do we start?"

Mother looks at Sebastian and gives him a nod. Sebastian starts walking across the room towards the cabinet. Mother gets my attention by snapping her fingers and says "These new abilities won't come easy and they will take time to master, but until then you need to protect yourself from what's coming." She waves Sebastian over and he hands me the weapon I was checking out just days earlier.

Sebastian seems a little reluctant to pass the weapon over at first and then releases his grip. Standing close to me he begins pointing out and describes what it is that I'm holding isn't just some odd mash-up of hardware. Sebastian says "Listen, and listen good. This isn't some toy that you can play around with. This is a serious weapon."

As I look over the gun I finally got to have in my hands I say "Yeah, yeah. I got it. Not a toy"

Sebastian snatches the shotgun back from me so fast it didn't even give me a chance to protest. He says "There are things you need to know about it to truly understand what you think you are holding."

Looking me dead in my eyes he continues "This is a Winchester lever action model 1901 that fires 10 gauge shells. Those shells are loaded with special shot that has been blessed, so don't waste them. This weapon was carried during World War I by a Navajo code talker. He was lost behind enemy lines alone. He fought his way through platoon after platoon to return to his base untouched. The ax that is on the end was forged from the three nails of the cross that held Jesus for his crucifixion. They were discovered as part the emperor of Constantinople's helmet and horses bridle. This combined makes it an evil destroying machine."

It took me a moment to regain my speech and pick my jaw up from the floor. Before reaching for the shotgun I wiped the sweat from my hands on my shirt. Gently I take the weapon from Sebastian and say "I don't know what to say other than holy hell! Something like this will come in handy."

I eye the shotgun still awestruck of what I was holding and say "I feel like I need to smite something, babe look at this thing."

Jenny not sure of what's going on and still waiting for the explanation of the dream says "That's lovely, I got five bucks says you either shoot yourself or cut yourself before weeks end."

I reach out to shake her hand and say "No faith, you're on." While pulling my hand back I bump the blade of the ax and slice my forearm. I look at Jenny with a beaten look on my face of embarrassment say "I'll pay you when we get back to the apartment."

Mother and Jenny laugh as I look at the cut. I set the weapon on the table so I don't further injure myself. Jacqueline gets up to find some bandages to clean the wound. I look over to find Sebastian shaking his head in utter disbelief that I managed to hurt myself within minutes of having this thing.

When Jacqueline returned with some gauze I pulled my blood soaked sleeve up to expose to wound. She wiped the area with a towel to clear away the blood to assess the severity of the cut. With the amount of blood on my shirt I knew it had to be pretty bad. After pressing and holding the towel to the area for a moment she removed it to see if the blood had stopped only to find split in the skin exposing more of the black onyx like skin. The pitch black skin didn't even have a mark from the blade. Everyone in the room looked at the wound in amazement.

I look closely at the newly exposed skin trying to figure out why it wasn't damaged as well. I must have been focusing pretty hard because I was startled when Mother yelled "Sebastian don't" I looked up just in time to see Sebastian swinging the ax blade downward at my arm. Frozen in fear I wasn't able to pull my arm back fast enough. The blade hit the fresh black skin with so much impact that the table shook violently. I was afraid I just lost my arm from just below the elbow I couldn't even convince myself to open my eyes. The fear faded slowly away as I heard Sebastian laugh. I looked down at my arm to find nothing wrong with the new skin.

I pull my arm back off the table just in case he decided to try it again and say "Very funny asshole, hitting the table instead of me. Way to make a guy almost piss himself."

Jenny leans towards me and in a very serious voice says "He did hit your arm, not the table." She was making a swinging motion with her hand like she was chopping to show me where it hit. Mother backhands Sebastian in the stomach, not very hard just enough that he would know he did something he shouldn't have. Sebastian stopped laughing and straightened up and said "Sorry, it was the only way to show you that it couldn't actually hurt you."

A little taken back by Sebastian's statement I say " You could've just told me. I would've believed you, but NOOOOOO you had to try and freak me out."

"I think I did more than try to scare you" Sebastian said with a chuckle.

Mother shot both of us a look to knock it off and said "Sebastian would you like to explain to them why there was no harm done?"

Sebastian nodded his head yes and said "The blade will damage your so called human flesh because that part is mortal. It won't damage the black skin because that is of the old gods. You do know you are a demigod, correct? It has its advantages at times."

A little intrigued and a whole lot relieved I look over the ax blade. It took me a second before something hit me and I could tell Jenny was having the same thought. I knew she was when she said "Wait, if it can't hurt his black-god-skin or whatever you want to call it then how did they nail Jesus to the cross with them? He was supposed to be the son of God right?"

Mother thought about it for a moment and said "Well that's another story. He wasn't a demigod exactly, he was more of a descendant of the tribes cross breeding."

"What the fuck, are you saying the bible and religion thing is all bogus?" Jenny says now lost like her world has just crumbled.

Mother thinking of what to say and trying to choose her words carefully. Finally she said "People try to explain things the best they know how. At the time everyone was trying to say their religion was better than the next. Most of the gifted remained off the radar and didn't want to draw any attention to themselves or their families."

Jenny and I locked eyes in shock. It's not an easy thing to deal with when your entire thought process of the world has been crushed. After a few minutes of awkward silence I said the only words that would form "Wow, consider my mind blown." Looking over at Jenny I say "Hey babe, are you okay over there?"

Jenny sat back and ran her hand through her hair in what looked like frustration and said "I need a breather for a few to let all this sink in." She got up from her chair slowly and walked out of the room.

Sitting in my chair holding the weapon in my hand as the new reality slowly soaks in I question everything that I know. What is real and what is a story that someone made up to appease the masses? So many lies, so many half-truths are told by millions daily. I'm lost on who to believe anymore. This all too much for one person to take at once.

Just as I feel I'm starting to get a grip on my sanity again Sebastian walks up to me and hands me a strip of leather approximately three and half feet long. Now I'm confused again and say "What's this for, is it some magical binding leather or something like that?"

Sebastian gave me a look of me being the densest person on the planet and says "No, it's just a piece of leather you could use as a sling. I found it on the floor over there. Sebastian pointed to an area in the corner that had piled of damaged books. He chuckled and said "Not everything is special, sometimes a string is just a string."

Feeling even stupider than normal I say "Thanks for the philosophy lesson Sigmund Freud."

Sebastian shakes his head and says "He was a psychologist not a philosopher dumbass."

Getting agitated I shift in my chair and point at Sebastian and say "You know what, I liked you better when you didn't talk so much."

That bothered Sebastian and he started towards me. To be ready for anything he might come at me with I stood up quick to show him I wasn't afraid of him. Mother slammed her hand onto the table causing us both to stand down.

Without missing a beat Sebastian and I simultaneously said "He started it"

Mother put her hand to her head bowing it slightly and said "like dealing with small children" She looked at Jacqueline and said "Do you see what I've been putting up with?"

Still standing I start heading to the doorway when mother asks me "where are you going? Sit down, there's no reason to leave."

I turn to face mother and say "I'm not leaving, I'm just going to check on Jenny. I need to see if she's alright."

Mother nods her head in acknowledgment and says "Good idea, she's processing more information than she should have to."
I walk through the doorway and make my way to the storefront. Its slow moving with the dim lighting, trying not to trip on the clutter of oddities. I see her silhouette near the front window. Knowing where I need to go to I plan my way through the room. When I'm within five feet of her I call out her name so I don't startle her. She looks back slightly over her shoulder and says "Take a look at this."

I can see that she is focusing on something outside on the street but can't see what it is right away till I get behind her. I wrap my arms around her waist from behind and say "I'm sorry about all of this. It's new to me as well."

She reaches up and grabs my chin, turning it to where she is looking and says "Yeah, yeah, shut up and look at this."

I try to see what she sees and a say "What are we looking at?" It took me less than thirty seconds before I noticed the movement between the building. There's at least fifteen men without shirts gathered together. I can see the rune tattoos covering their torsos. "OH SHIT, GET IN THE BACK NOW!"

Not caring what I knock over or step on we run to the back room. I keep Jenny in front of me just in case someone was to bust in the front guns blazing. At least I could potentially shield her. We run through the curtains of the backroom without slowing and I almost plow in Sebastian. Not entirely sure what I plan on doing I grab the shotgun and start looking for the ammo. Jenny short of breath from our sprint stands by the table.

Not really talking to anyone specific I say "Ammo, where is the ammo?"

My actions caused everyone in the room to go on high alert. Sebastian moved to the curtains peering through a small opening. Mother grabs hold of my arm while I'm frantically pacing the floor and says "What is it, what's happening?"

I stop for a moment and slow my breathing so I can make sense to them and say "I'm pretty sure shit is about to hit the fan." The confused and concerned faces that stared back at me told me I should elaborate. "We just saw about fifteen or so shirtless rune covered goons across the street gathering in the alley. Either they are about to make their way over here and finish what they started or they are having the strangest book club meeting of all time and I'm fairly certain most of them can't read."

I look back to where Sebastian was and find him gone. A moment later he comes through the curtain and heads straight for the shelf in the corner. Sebastian grabs something off of the third shelf and tosses it at me. Once I catch it I realize it's a box of shotgun shells. I start loading round after round when Sebastian says "I count sixteen and they are armed with knives and bats, so aim low and take out the legs. They are heading this way so Jacqueline, take mother and Jenny to the safe room. Jacob and I can handle them."

I kiss Jenny as they head for the safe room and say "Don't come out till I tell you it's safe." Mother pulls jenny into the room and as Jacqueline closes the door. I hear the door seal and lock just as the glass on the front door shatters. I lay the remaining shotgun shells on the table so I can grab them when I run out and give Sebastian a reassuring look that we got this. I see Sebastian reach behind his back and pull a mace like club made from bone out from under his jacket.

He could see the surprise on my face and gave me a grin as the first of the goons made their way through the door frame.

Without a word I point and fired the shotgun. The echo filled the room as the shot hit the man dead center of his chest. The watery splatter of the blood sprayed outward coating the faces of the next two combatants. This gave Sebastian time to close the gap. Swinging the bone mace at the jawbone of the number two man. The impact was almost as loud as the shotgun blast. On a backswing Sebastian caught the third man right behind his right ear.

Sebastian stepped out from in front of the doorway to give me a clear shot at the next round of goons. There was a hesitation on the other side of the curtain and I could make out the sounds of the first three being dragged out of the way.

After waiting for a full minute after the dragging sound stopped of silence I took the time to add a shotgun shell to top off the weapon. I can only assume the sound of me chambering a round prompted our assailants to rethink their strategy of coming in in force. To further hammer home that we aren't going down easy I fired a shot off into the left side of the curtain since that was the way they would have to funnel in here from the front. Upon chambering, I heard a familiar voice speak up, it was Fred.

Fred's voice was shaking and unsure but he was trying hard to cover his nervousness with laughter saying "Hey now, hey now. We just want to talk."

Trying to listen closely of where exactly along the wall Fred's voice was coming from I figured if I could keep him talking it could by us time. Signaling with my hands to Sebastian to shift over some I say to Fred "Sorry, stores closed for repairs. Some wannabe little sheep busted in the front door. Maybe you saw them, kinda squirrelly looking, shirtless with some stupid tattoos." I knew irritating a gang of thugs hell bent on destruction may not have been the best option but what the hell. If it's one thing I learned taking care of myself all these years it's an angry man is more prone to screw up.

I knew I that my comment got under his skin when Fred's voice came back slightly louder and more agitated saying "WHO ARE YOU CALLING WANNABES?"

Sebastian shot me a slight grin of approval knowing my plan was working. I needed to keep this going and maybe Fred will slip up and give us something we can use, whether it be against him or his master. I couldn't resist chuckling as I said "Did I hurt your little feelings? You were the one that wanted to talk, so talk."

I could hear Fred taking deep breaths, probably in an attempt to calm down. The creek of the hardwood floor came from the other side of the curtain about midway of the door frame. I aimed low so I could hopefully get a leg shot and fired. A scream came from the other side and a thump of a body hitting the floor. Groaning and sliding sounds soon followed as the goon drug himself out from in front of the doorway. Fred screamed out "STOP SHOOTING!" he lowered his voice as I chambered another round and said "He wasn't trying anything. He just was trying to check on his brother."

Knowing that the bad guy count has gone from sixteen to twelve and our odds were growing ever so slightly I say "Sorry, that was my bad. New toy and all. Honestly I didn't know the trigger was so touchy."

After some shuffling and mumbling beyond the curtain Fred cleared his throat and said "Look truce, I'm coming in there to talk face to face." Not sure if Fred just grew some massive balls or if he was aware of how monumentally stupid of an idea this actually was. The call of "I'm unarmed and coming in."

I assume our silence was a sign of agreement to Fred but the curtains began to open. Fred walked slowly through with both hands open and outstretched. Once he was through the doorway he completed a slow turn to prove he had nothing behind his back or tucked in his pants. His eyes locked on Sebastian during his spin. After a brief awkward moment of eye contact with my massive partner Fred said "You are freaking huge"

Sebastian postured from his hunched fighting stance and gave a priceless reply "Arm or Ribs?" The confusion on Fred's face indicated he didn't know what was coming.

Since Fred didn't answer I felt it was my duty to help the situation resolve itself to my favor and said "I vote ribs, he's a decent drummer and can still play if you leave his arms." Without hesitation Sebastian took advantage of Fred's raised arm and with a quick swing caught the man in the rib cage with the mace.

Fred crumpled to the floor in agony to breathless to even scream. When he regained his use of word, even as labored as they were Fred said "I thought we had a truce"

I smirked, keeping the shotgun trained on him and said "You called truce, I never agreed." I lowered the weapon slightly to indicate I was going to comply and said "Now we can have that truce, grab a seat and we can have that talk."

He climbed to his feet using the chair for balance and lowered himself down careful to avoid hitting his ribs on the high arm rests. I chose the chair on the left of the table for the tactical advantage. First it gives me clear view of the doorway and second I'm far enough away to void a lunge if he feels froggy.

The pain must be intense for Fred from the look on his face as he shifted to get comfortable. I sat ready but relaxed with the shotgun resting on my leg with the barrel pointed towards the door. Sebastian stayed to the left of the doorway watching for any movement that might be threatening. The tension in the room was thick and my thoughts drifted to the three women hiding in the safe room. I'm unaware if Fred and the acolytes of darkness know they are in there or not with all of the wards that are on that thing.

The silence was killing me because I didn't trust Fred not to just be here stalling me while his minions prepared for round two so I decided to speak up and say "You've had your chances to talk for days now and haven't. You just stood there and watched. What is so important that you want to break your creeper gaze now and be civilized?"

Still moving slow from his fresh injury Fred sat upright. He flinched and braced for impact when Sebastian shifted his stance. When he was sure he wasn't going to get clobbered again he said "The master bids me to do this" Fred closes his eyes and takes a deep breath to clear is mind. When he regains composure he says "The master sent me to give you a message. He would like to meet on neutral ground."

Feeling uneasy myself now, I reply in a sarcastic tone "If that's all it was why didn't you just leave a note under my door or some shit instead of busting in here like Elliot Ness."

Fred started to raise his hand and stopped when he saw Sebastian move closer. Lowering his hand back to the armrest he said "He wasn't sure you would come if we didn't prove we are serious about this meeting. This is not a request it's a summons."

I'm not sure if I should be offended or honored that he would send so many people after me so I had to ask "First of I don't think you are in any position to demand anything, second and most important how positive are you that the rest of you will walk out of here."

Fred had fear in his eyes with the revelation that he could die at any moment and put both hands up in a defensive position and said "Please don't, the master sent an offering."

I was consumed by intrigue instantly. It made my mind race wondering what he could possibly give me that would make me want to meet with Akhkharu after he's tried to kill me once before. I didn't want to alert him of my curiosity so I asked in a coy manner "So where is this so called offering, and what is it?"

Fred concerned for his safety with what he was about to say was evident and said "If you would allow one of my guys to come in, he needs to carry it. He will come in sit it down and leave without trying anything."

Sebastian tightened his grip on his mace and seemed to be itching to use it again. From the look on his face I would assume he missed combat. There's no telling what he's been through but this made him happy. Know that Sebastian was ready I said "Okay, send in your guy with this thing. Be warned if he tries anything he die where he stands."

Fred turned a little to face the door raising his voice said "Joseph, bring in the offering and don't try anything stupid. They aren't playing around."

All of our attentions were on the door. Sebastian in a batter's stance with his mace, my left hand gripped the front of the short barrel while my right hand rested close to the trigger. A man I can only assume was Joseph entered the room toting a small black leather bound chest approximately two feet long, eight inches tall and ten inches wide. He walked slower once he noticed Sebastian was ready to take of his head.

Joseph took careful steps forward and slowly set the chest on the table and took a step backwards. I sat up in my chair leaning just a hair forward to get a better look at this box. The markings carved in it were like nothing I've seen before. With all the recent research I thought I would have come across these designs at some point. They almost resembled pictographs in a way.

With my attention on the black chest, Joseph took that moment to try to lean down to tell Fred something. When he tapped Fred on the ribs the wince of pain made Sebastian swing for the fences. The crack the club made upon contact with Joseph's head reminded me of an old video of Hank Aaron hitting a homerun. Josephs corpse flew back, making its way through the curtain. This action caused more of the acolytes to file in like lambs to slaughter. Fred fell face down to the floor putting his hands over his head showing he wasn't a threat.

Taking turns between me shooting and Sebastian crushing bones the goons fell. When no more of them entered for a full five minutes Sebastian and I looked at each other not knowing what came next. I took the time to reload the shotgun and count my remaining shells, only have seven left from the box. I tried to count in my head how many I had fired but couldn't recall exactly with how fast it all happened. Sebastian stood silent as always wiping the gore from his bone mace. He still had a faint smile lingering from his thrill of open combat. They barely had a chance to fight back with how blindly they rushed in.

I survey the cluster of bodies to try and get an accurate count of the carnage. We don't want any surprise attacks from one of these freaks. They seem so willing to die for a cause that I won't ever truly understand. After counting I decided to recount just to know my numbers were correct I yell to the room "Hey big man, how many did you say we're out here?"

Sebastian stopped cleaning off his toy and thought and says "Sixteen I believe, why?"

Recounting for a third time, I say "I'm missing one. There's only fifteen out here, do you think one took off running out of here?"

Sebastian stuck his head out to the hallway through the tattered curtain and did a quick count and said "I assume it's possible that one got away, if he did we can only hope he learned a lesson."

Coming back into the back room I step over and around the bodies littering the floor when I realize why my count was off. I spot Fred hiding under the table in the fetal position. I sling my shotgun over my shoulder and reach down under the table towards Fred and tap his leg to get his attention and say "Fred, get your ass out here."

Fred swats at my hand in protest and in a trembling voice says "No, you're just going to kill me."

I hold back the laughter as I stand up and unsling the shotgun. I take the weapon over to the shelf and set it down then walk back towards the table. I say "Seriously, I will not kill you. I'm unarmed."

Fred lifts his head to look around seeing that I no longer have a gun pointed at him. He notices Sebastian near the door engrossed in his inspection of the maces that Fred starts hesitantly making his way from under the table. He resembled a scolded dog, afraid at any moment he could receive another beating.

I took a step back to give Fred some breathing room. I knew he wouldn't try to make a run for it with Sebastian standing near the only exit. I motioned for him to take a seat as I pulled up a chair for myself. Fred sat still skittish but he showed some sign of believing that he was safe from at least me. He eyed my shotgun that lay on the shelf just four feet from me. I could see in his eyes that he knew there was no way he could clear the distance before I could, so he moved his attention to me.

Seeing how uneasy Fred looked was a little confidence booster with this being my first real standoff. Sure I run my mouth a lot, but most people see all the scars and back off. I'm not totally convinced it's as much fear as it's taking pity of the messed up guy. I lean back and prop my legs up on a box hoping it will help Fred to calm down and maybe give up some much needed information. From the look on his face I knew something wasn't going as planned. Fred pointed at the sole of my work boots. I pulled my foot towards my chest to see what freaked him out to find an eyeball squished between the treads. I must have got it stuck when I was in the hall counting. Since my approach seemed to be failing no matter what I did I decided to just cut to the chase and say "First off Fred, may I call you Fred?" Fred slowly nodded his head in approval. "Okay Fred, I want to tell you that causing a bloodbath in a bookstore is not what I wanted to do today." Placing my hands to my chest I say "I would like to offer you an apology and condolences for all of your friends."

Fred's eyes still scanning the grizzly scene and says "They weren't friends exactly, I didn't even meet half of them until an hour ago."

Leaning back again I put my legs back up on the box without thinking of the eye. I notice his eyes drift back to my feet so I say "Fred, up here." Waving my hands so he makes eye contact. "We need to focus on the task at hand. That task is your master and what he wants. Which brings us to the box."

We both look at the leather bound chest on the table. I stand up to make my way to the chest and when I get to the table I say "Is this a trap Fred? It's not going to explode when I open it, or is it full of venomous snakes coiled and ready to attack?"

Fred shakes his head no and says "Honestly, I have no clue what's in the damn thing. The person who would've known had his head taken off by Bigfoot over there." As he pointed to Sebastian.

I must admit Sebastian did seem like he was enjoying himself a little too much as he was crushing bones. So I turn back to Fred and lean back slightly propping myself up against the table and say "So what are we going to do with you Freddie ole pal?" Not giving him a chance to respond I continue "we can't just let you leave knowing you might come back later. I suppose we could cripple you to where you couldn't do anything but eat through a straw for the rest of your life."

Before Fred could say anything to plead his case Sebastian spoke up saying "My vote is for the crippling thing."

I start pacing the room and say "Well that's one vote for crippling, and I'm still undecided so what's your vote Fred?"

The way Fred was squirming combined with the faces he was making had me convinced that I had him right where I needed him to be. I motioned to Fred to answer the question and he says "There has got to be another option, come on." If I wouldn't have been looking at him as he said it, I would think he was on his knees begging. I pretended to think it over, scratching my chin. That was until I realized I had gotten a little goon goo on my hand from blow back splatter.

I wipe my hand off on my pant leg and walk back to Fred saying "Okay, I will give you a chance to tell me why I should stop the big man from going full chimpanzee on you." The second it came out of my mouth I realized I might have gone a step too far. It was solidified when Sebastian gave me a horrified look.

It seemed to work and push Fred in the right direction when he spoke up saying "What if I work for you and get information for you on Akhkharu?"

Sebastian shrugged his shoulders showing me this was all my decision. Knowing this could go two way, horribly wrong or very helpful I felt optimistic. "Alright, say I let you slide and you become our snitch how should this work? Should we make you learn a secret language or get burner phones so they can't trace it?"

For once Fred seemed annoyed with me instead of scared. He slowly stood up, keeping an eye on Sebastian. "Why don't I just knock on your door and tell you? Remember I live across the hall from you and you brutally murdered my roommate." He says pointing to the man with a hole the size of a softball in his chest.

I look over at the heap of flesh lying half out of the room and say "Oh yeah, I thought he looked familiar. That would work as well, see you are already helping" I pat him on the back as I walk by. "We have to make it look like you barely got away so it's more believable." Sebastian assumed that was his cue and backhands Fred in the jaw sending him flying a few feet before crashing into the bookshelves.

Fred laying on the floor in a daze props himself up on his left arm says "You didn't have to do that. You already busted my ribs to hell." He remained on the floor nursing his wounds away from Sebastian's reach.

I look at Sebastian in surprise and say "That was awesome, but he was right. I mean you did fuck up his ribs pretty bad. Remind me later to talk to you about how much you are enjoying this." Shaking my head not believing that just happened I walked over to Fred and offer him a hand up.

I get Fred to his feet and walk him out of the back room and down the hallway to the main store and explain that he needs to get out of here and I will be expecting an update from him tomorrow on what Akhkharu is wanting to do.

Making my way to the back I start thinking of the mess of bodies and the busted front door. At some point someone had to have called the cops, if not for the gaggle of men kicking in the front door and rushing in the gunfire had to alert at least one person. I stood silent and listened for a few minutes and heard nothing. There were no sirens, no traffic, no barking dogs, there was absolutely no sounds. Jacqueline had said before that this building was warded but I guess I never truly understood what that meant until now.

I had to shake it off and get back there and see what's in the box. As I pass the curtains I hear Sebastian talking to Mother. I see Jacqueline signaling for Jenny to stay in the safe room so I say "Hey Jenny, it's a mess out here. You're going to want to stay back till we get this cleaned up a bit."

Jenny sneaks passed Jacqueline when she wasn't watching and said "It can't be that bad." Stopping mid-sentence to cover her mouth in terror from the amount of carnage that lay near the doorway. I rush over to Jenny, not sure what to do other than block her from seeing the mess. I turn her away from the mass of bodies and try to pull her close. She pushes back and points towards the door and yells "YOU DID THIS! WHAT, WHY"

Feeling lost and now consumed with fear that I might have just drove her away I hung my head and said "To protect you, they ran in ready for war." I stepped back from her and walked way to help Sebastian clear the bodies from the hallway. Jacqueline was leading us down the hall to a door. I knew jenny was going to need time to process this and maybe Mother can help. I get to the door and notice the stairs going down to a basement.

Sebastian goes down first and I follow, leaving the body behind. I don't need to attempt to carry something down and kill myself in the process. When I get to the basement I see Sebastian loading one of the corpses into a giant furnace so I tell say to Sebastian "Hey, you stay down here and toss them in and I will go up there and push them down the stairs. It will go faster that way and get them out of the hallway for now." Sebastian gives me the thumbs up and I head back up stairs.

I do my best to refrain from looking in on Jenny but I just had to know how she was. Looking through a hole in the curtain I see her sitting in the corner sobbing. Mother catches me watching and waves me off so I grab the next body and drag it to the stairs.

Bloody corpse after bloody corpse I line them up at the top of the stairs awaiting Sebastian to give me the signal to kick another down. The thudding and wet thump as they tumble is a bit unnerving, but a few let out groans. I not entirely sure if it was just gases leaving the body or if they were still alive. Sebastian took care of those with a final blow to each ones skull before he drag them to the furnace.

Looking back as I waited I saw Jacqueline spraying some horrible smelling cleaner on the blood pools and walls. As the last of the goons tumbled down the stairs I went to help scrub up the mess I help create. With me scrubbing and her mopping the blood mostly vanished. This took a good thirty minutes before Jacqueline took the mop and scrub brush and went to her living area of the store and returned with a picture in a frame and a throw rug to cover what we couldn't manage to get rid of.

Jacqueline made her way into the back room and stopped to hold the curtain aside for me but I waved her on so I could give Jenny the space I feel she needs. This time alone gave me a chance to reflect myself on how fast the events unfolded. I try to figure out why I remained so calm and the situation didn't rattle me. With this being the first time I've ever shot someone it felt instinctive and almost natural. The realization of the fact that killing came natural made me shudder. What kind of monster have I become, what kind of monster could do this to people?

The thoughts burrow deep into my head, grabbing hold of my memories. Memories that I thought long gone were making their way to the surface. Some of them I don't recognize or wouldn't believe if I wasn't seeing them through my own eyes. The people were familiar but I had to be no more than an infant. I see my parents and I see Mother. At that moment deep in thought I'm startled by Sebastian patting me on the shoulder to check on me.

Sebastian pulling open the curtain says "Come on, let's see what's so important in that chest."

I had forgotten all about the chest in the frenzy of the past hour. Try to collect myself and I follow Sebastian into the room glancing in Jenny's direction. The crying has stopped and Jacqueline was sitting next to her whispering softly. Mother gave me a nod and started toward me saying "So what happened that caused all this?"

Standing next to the table staring down at the chest I say "Well they gave me this thing as an offering from Akhkharu, so I will meet him on neutral ground. And then as you can tell all hell broke loose."

Mother walked closer to examine the outside of the black leather bound chest giving the appearance that she recognized it. She ran her fingers along the length of it and traced the design that was carved in the edges. After a moment she looked up and says "This is no regular offering, I haven't seen this in a very long time. Akhkharu must know that I am working with you for it to deliver something such as this."

Confused and concerned I ask "What is it and why do I feel I should be worried right now? My eyes big with the anticipation of the answer.

I could tell from her face that Mother didn't know where to begin. The only way to describe her expression was a combination of fear and sadness. Sebastian went to her side to give her support and offer comfort. When she composed herself enough to speak she cleared her throat and said "This chest dates back to the beginning. To the time of the Old gods Tiamat and Apsu. Through them other gods were born. This chest is made from one of those gods, Apsu. It contains the history of the events written on the flesh of the fallen generals. I'm sorry I can't finish."

As Sebastian led Mother away from the chest to sit I turned the chest towards me. The latch and handles didn't appear to be metal but more like stone. The lock just hung in place open and unsecured. I removed the lock and took a deep breath before opening the lid. Feeling prepared for what I might find I flipped the latch and as I started to raise the lid, Jenny's hand slid on top of mine stopping me. I turned to her, locking eyes. A veil of despair cloaked the normal spark in her eyes. I could see that there were more important things than what lies in the chest. I took in a glance of Mother, there was something that she knows that she refuses to tell me. Sebastian seems to know what's wrong but I feel it's probably best not to push right now.

Looking back at Jenny I quietly say "Later, the chest can wait until later." Hugging her gently appeared to calm her down, because the trembling is barely noticeable. As I walked with Jenny to help comfort Mother I hear Jacqueline behind me say "It's empty, they offered you an empty box."

Mother sat up and wiped the tears from her eyes, I turned to go see what Jacqueline was talking about. Unaware of how Mother made it to the table before I had and was already inspecting the inside of the chest. The way she was checking the edges I would guess there was a hidden panel. As she ran her fingers around the base there was an audible click. Mother opened the now slightly ajar panel fully and pulled what looked like a blood cover scroll from the compartment.

The look of total disgust was present on Mothers face. The blood looked somewhat fresh, sticky and tacky to the touch. Mother looked for a place to unroll the dripping scroll. I found a cardboard box in the corner and grabbed the lid. As I was bringing it back to the table, jenny saw what I was doing and cleared a spot for the lid to fit.

Mother laid out the scroll unrolling as she went. The blood was congealed and looked more like red syrup than anything. Once it was fully unraveled we could see this scroll was fresh human flesh that was carved off of someone and used as parchment. Jacqueline picked up the cleaning spray and a towel from the chair and began spraying off Mother's hands as well as the marked up flesh.

Jacqueline wiped carefully so the markings wouldn't smear at first, that was until I took a closer look and noticed the markings weren't written but tattooed into the flesh. Imaging whether this person that gave this amount of flesh was willing or not and if the tattoo was done first or after it was stripped from its host made me cringe.

With the flesh cleaned I attempted to read what was scribbled on it with no luck. Mother took a glance around me while she was drying her hands. Without a word she took hold of my wrist and placed my left hand directly on the tattooed flesh. As my hand covered those images I understood what was there, it was a message from Akhkharu. My eyes still closed as the words hung there in my mind I say "Quick one of you grab something to write on and a pen. Tell me when you are ready to copy this down."

I hear the rustling of papers for the frantic search for a moment then I hear Jenny say "Okay, got it. Ready when you are."

Focusing on the words I read them as the pass by "We are to meet when the light and dark occupy the same place outside where we last battled. Come alone and unarmed as will I." As I read the last word aloud the flesh burst into flames consuming all trace that it existed. I pulled my hand just as the flames started causing me to singe the hair from my hand.

My eyesight returned blurry at first, I assume because this is only the second time I've tried to use this new skill. Jenny saw how unsteady I looked and held me by placing her arm around my waist to provide balance. I worked my way to the nearest chair sitting less than gracefully down smacking the back of my head on the high back of the chair. Gripping Jenny's hand softly I pulled her to me having her sit on my lap so I could hold her.

Everyone just looked at each other not wanting to address the instructions that were given. Mother stood near the table consumed by worry, Sebastian seemed to be coming down from his clobbering high or whatever it was. Jacqueline acted like she wanted to say something but nothing came out and jenny just sat there on my lap with her head on my shoulder silent. I had no choice but to speak up and say "We need to break it down in sections to try and figure out what it means."

Jenny still held the paper in her hand, lifted her head and said "well we can only assume that it mean outside the house where you saved me."

"Okay good that's one part done. Let me see here, the come alone and unarmed part is pretty self-explanatory. Now all we need to do is figure out this first part." I say feeling optimistic that we can get it deciphered.

Jacqueline reaches for the paper and takes it from Jenny and reads "We are to meet when the light and dark occupy the same place. The only thing that comes to mind is a solar eclipse. Those don't happen that often but there is one in two days."

Mother shakes her head yes to what Jacqueline said, and starts looking on the table for something. Within seconds she finds a book and flips it open, scanning page after page till she says "It was right here all along. See look" pointing to a section halfway down the page. Mothers excitement showed as she read "When the darkness of night conquers the light of day the dark ones lose their power and become normal for that brief moment in time. So if this is correct he will be stuck powerless in human form as long as the eclipse is in full effect."

Jenny still sitting on my lap took hold of my chin turning my head to face her, she stared directly into my eyes and said "I know what you're thinking and the answer is no! I'm not going to let you take on this thing alone." I started to respond when she pinched my lips closed and said "I didn't say you could talk yet. Just because some old book says something doesn't mean it's true. I think it's a trap if you ask me." She lets go of my chin and lays her head back on my shoulder as she says "You can talk now."

I look at Mother who was grinning from how Jenny just took charge. Thinking things through was giving me a headache. It could be the fact that I haven't eaten anything since breakfast so I propose that we order something as we try to come up with a plan.

Jenny received a call from her work while we were arguing over what to eat. They wanted her to come in for a shift. Her being by herself right now with everything going on bothered me, but she assured me that she would be fine and check in throughout her shift. That eased my worries ever so slightly. I know she can take care of herself and has for years, also knowing what's out there now makes you more aware of what to watch for.

I borrowed Jacqueline's car to give Jenny a ride back to the apartment so she could get her car. I watch her fire up the beast and rev the engine a few times to help warm up the engine, her driver's door closed and she drove off. Before heading back to the bookstore I decided to run up to my apartment and grab a few thing that I might need. I can hear Fred moaning through his door as I'm opening mine, causing me to chuckle. Sebastian did knock the hell out of him.

While inside my place I grabbed my phone charger and a different shirt. I didn't need to advertise I'm even more of a freak than people thought running around with blood splatter decorating my wardrobe. On my way out I remember the shot gun, I'm going to need to conceal it somehow, and get a brilliant idea. I open the hallway closet door and snatch the over-sized zip up hoodie hanging there and put it on. It's big enough to hide it and not too heavy where I'm going to sweat my ass off all day.

As I locked my door I started feeling bad for Fred, so I thought I would check in on him. I knocked on the door and heard Fred's pain filled voice yell "It's open!"

Entering I see the piles of boxes spread across the room. Fred was standing over an opened box, his ribs were wrapped up from where Sebastian had delivered a crushing blow. As he turned I could see he had a large blood soaked bandage covering his chest. Once he saw it was me, he made his way to the windows and closed the blinds.

I stayed put in the doorway, until all the blinds facing his boss's house were closed. As the final blind closed he turned to me saying "What do you want, here to beat on me some more?"

I shake my head no and take a step closer and say "Nah, that's not how I do things. I'm just here to check on you. Obviously something else happened after you left, are you okay?" I point to the seeping bandage covering most of his chest.

Fred looks down seeing the blood says "Oh this, this was a punishment from the master for allowing so many of our people to get slaughtered" He walked across to the couch and picked up his shirt. As he carefully attempted to pull his shirt over his head I could tell the ribs were hurting more than he wanted me to know.

I didn't want to let him know that I knew how bad he was busted up but I couldn't just leave him hung up with his shirt on his head. I reached forward grabbing his shirt tail and pulling it down for him. I took a step back so I wasn't crowding him and I said "Look, I know what you are going through with that claw mark," I pulled my shirt collar to the side to reveal the scar on my shoulder. "See, he got me too."

Fred gets a closer look at my scar and says "Shit, is mine going to turn black too? That thing looks nasty"

I laugh a little at the thought and say "No, long story short I'm not exactly normal. That's my other skin or whatever they want to call it."

Fred wiped off his forehead in relief as he says "That's good at least, well for me anyway. I'll be alright I guess, just trying to get this place livable for now."

"Alright" I say as I make my way to the door. "You know how to find me if you need anything. I'm not saying let's be best buds but we can at least try not to kill each other for a while, deal."

"Deal" Fred says as he starts sorting through another box. I head back to Jacqueline's car and make my way back to the bookstore. The thought crosses my mind that last time I was late to food Sebastian ate most of it, leaving me just enough to make me hungrier.

With all that is going on I just want to clear the thoughts that are torturing me. I dig through Jacqueline's music selection if that's what you she wants to call in and come up with nothing helpful. I guess the music is going to have to wait for another day when time is plentiful and worries not clouding every aspect of my day.

Thinking back as I drive slowly back the store that things would be so much easier if I was normal. I couldn't remember a time that this so called gift has actually made my life less stressful, from the testing to the endless foster and state homes, the names being muttered under people's breath. Then again I've always been good about self-sabotage and blowing off my responsibilities. Leaving the mess for others to clean up. Maybe it's time to man up and finish something for once. This realization hit me as I pulled in a parking spot near the store. I was feeling a little better on the outlook of the upcoming events I grabbed my charger and got out of the car.

My mind must have drifted a little too far because as I walked through the busted front door I was stopped by a rather angry looking and large member of Kansas City's finest saying "Where do you think you are going?"

Caught off guard by the officers presence, I didn't know exactly what to say so I blurted out the first thing that came to mind "I'm here for my book club meeting." Looking around I notice that I walked passed three other officers and two squad cars before someone stopped me.

The officer looked even angrier now and in the most sarcastic tone possible says "Well as you can see, the place is closed for renovations and you're going to have to find a new place to hold book club."

I see Sebastian over the officer's shoulder signaling me to go around to the back of the store so I slowly back away from the officer and say "Chill, I'm sorry for bothering you. I wasn't paying attention and I can see you got your hands full. So I'm just going to get out of your hair."

I'm at least a dozen feet away when I hear the officer bellow "I don't want to see you cross that police tape again." Throwing my arm into the air with a big thumbs up I keep walking back to the car.

Once the officer's attention is off of me I make my way to the side of the building to meet Sebastian at the back door. When I get there not wanting to knock to alert the cops where I am, I text Mother that I'm there. She replied that there is a package hidden in a bag under a broken pallet near the wall. Digging through the debris I find Sebastian's' satchel. This bag has been crammed full with books and my shotgun. Taped to the strap I find a note explaining that the delivery driver called the cops and they will meet me at my place when everything is settled.

I leave the keys to Jacqueline's car on the back steps and text Mother where I put them. Knowing I can't walk back around holding a shotgun with all the cops standing around up front, I sneak down to the end of the alley. Sure it's out of my way but ending up in jail is not an option. Hidden by a few dumpsters I sling the shotgun over my shoulder and put my hoodie on to hid it. Positioning the satchel full of books over where my weapon hung to further hide it I feel it's time to move. I put my headphones in and hood up and walk.

The walk home gave me a much needed break from the fast paced hell that has happened lately. Keeping my head down to avoid attention I moved around the occasional groups of hipsters and the urban homeless.

Before I knew it I was only a block from home. Instead of going there I remembered I never got lunch. I went by the gas station at the end of the block and grabbed a couple sandwiches and an energy drink. On my way to the counter I thought about what all has transpired and thought this whole world might go to shit soon and I was going to need more caffeine than this little can could possibly offer.

I see Jessie behind the counter in the kitchen area and signal to him that I needed a boost. Jessie gives me a salute and turns to start making my special crack coffee, and I say "Make that two of them if you would kind sir."

Jessie turns in mid pour and says "Two, are you sure? I mean, I don't want to hear of your heart exploding"

I laugh as I make my way to the counter and say "Yes I'm sure. They aren't both for me, and if I do die from this I will make sure you aren't implicated in my passing."

Jessie turns back to the drink station and continues the masterpiece of caffeine saying "That's all needed to know. Two of them coming up."

I finally make it back my place and head inside. I take the satchel off my shoulder and toss it on the couch. I feel the instant relief from the extra weight of the bag the moment my grip released. I remember why I got the extra coffee and sandwich and head across the hall to Fred's place. I can't explain why I want to go over there other than curiosity, and we all know what it did to that damn cat. Hopefully I'm a little harder to kill than that poor feline, I test the water by kicking Fred's door a few times.

Fred yanks the door open and is surprised to see me standing there and says "What the hell do you want?"

I walk right passed him and began to make myself at home on the couch and say "I come baring lunch"

Fred noticeably put off by my brazen willingness to do as I please says "I can fend for myself on food, and another thing, you can't just barge in here."

I look over my shoulder at him as I take a bite of my sandwich and say with a mouthful of food "I doubt it, that oven hasn't worked in years. I've been meaning to fix it but never got around to it." I could see his frustration on his face as he slammed the door and made his way to the couch. "Actually I have other reasons to be here. I want to know what's up with this Akhkharu guy."

Fred shakes his head as he reaches for the sandwich and coffee saying "I don't know how I manage to get myself in these situations?"

Without looking up from my sandwich I say "no clue, but beware of that coffee. It has enough caffeine to kill an ox."

Fred takes off the lid of the coffee and sniffs it and says "I've drank worse things. By the way Akhkharu isn't a guy, or a chick for that matter. Akhkharu is one of the old gods."

I take a sip of my coffee to wash down the last bite then say "I know that, it's a lesser god of old or some shit. What I really want to know is why the dude hates me so much. For the most part before he showed up I kept to myself and never went out."

Fred sits back and unwraps his sandwich says "Honestly I have no clue what his plans are with you. We are pretty much left in the dark on all things. I did hear it say something about wanting you to reach your full potential first or your gift is pointless."

A sudden wave of understanding of what's going on hit me causing me to sit straight up and almost spill my drink in my lap. Everything was coming together piece by piece in my cluttered brain.

I jumped up and took off for my apartment stopping as I ran out the door. I went back in and grabbed my drink and say "Thanks for the chat, I got to do something."

As I was leaving again Fred yelled "HEY, WHEN ARE YOU GOING TO FIX MY OVEN?"

I turn and poke my head back in the door before I closed it and said "Dude, with everything going on right now you're worried about that thing. I will get to it next week, if your Master doesn't kill me first."

Now that I'm back in my apartment I ditch the hoodie and lay the shotgun on the couch next to me. Not being sure how long the bullshit at the bookstore is going to take I figure I've got a little time to kick off my boots and get comfortable while I go through the mound of books they packed up for me. After emptying the satchel out and assessing the stack it looks like I'm studying for some kind of midterm.

As I go over what Fred had said about Akhkharu only wanting the fully powered up people to devour I decided that starting in the book made from the black flesh is my best bet.

Page, after page of hidden text I read. It talks of the high gods and their failed plans, the lesser gods and their envy of the powers bestowed on the human filth. I'm halfway through when I find it, the tale of Akhkharu and his banishment from the city of the gods.

The book explains how Akhkharu and a few other lesser gods protested to the ruling King and Queen. Once the king had spoken that their decision was final a few of the lesser gods backed down and were forgiven for their outrage. Ereshkigal the goddess of the land of the dead stood side by side with Akhkharu until Tiamat announced the punishment. It was the harshest punishment a god could suffer, to have their powers removed and banishment to walk the earth as a mortal. Ereshkigal feared that she would one day have to suffer in the same pits of the dead that she controlled and sold out Akhkharu. She told Tiamat of the plan that Akhkharu had prepared and was released back to her realm. This infuriated Akhkharu, sending him into a rage. When his cult followers charged the palace it was all the distraction Akhkharu needed to make his escape. That's where the tale ends of Akhkharu.

With this new information, combined with what we already know about him I think there might be a way to exploit his rage. He can't have to many more goons running around here to willing to come after me after the massacre earlier today. Even if Fred was willing to come to his master's defense, he's too banged up to be a threat. Setting the books to the side I stand up to stretch and check the time. I take a look out of the window at the lot where Akhkharu currently resides. The house appears solid and not shifting. I make a mental note to ask Mother when she gets here if that's a good or bad thing. As I look over the house to find any sign of a weakness I notice the curtain of the window directly across from me is open. Even though the sun is shining directly in his window all I can see is pitch black.

I focus on the window, giving my eyes time to adjust when I hear the sound of Jenny's car rumbling down the street. As she parks, I look back to the window just as a massive clawed hand grabs the curtain and draws it closed. Was he watching me or was he waiting to see if I was alone. For all I know Akhkharu is just trying to cause doubt and catch me off guard. But from what Fred said that he wants me at full potential is the concerning part.

I hear the footsteps on the stairs of Jenny in her combat boots and before she gets to the door I yell "IT'S OPEN." I refused to take my eyes off the house when I hear the banging on my door. Making my way to the door, I say "I said it was open."

I opened the door to find Jenny standing there with two pizzas in her hands and her headphones in. Taking the pizzas from her to free up her hands, she removes one of her earbuds and says "What took you so long? Those are hot." Then she pushed herself passed me on her way to the couch.

Still standing in the doorway holding the food I turn and say "Hey babe, missed you too. How was work." I close the door with my foot and walk down the hallway to set the pizzas in the kitchen and join Jenny who is now lying slumped over on the couch. I sit on the end and pull her legs up onto my lap and untie boots. As I take them off I toss them in the corner with mine.

I rub Jenny's feet while she lays there and I ask "Long day at work?"

She shifts on the couch to lay on her back and says "Long day period, work sucked, but at least I got us some grub."

As I'm trying to help her relax I contemplate telling her what I figured out since she was gone. Also I think dropping on her that Fred and I had lunch together, that might send her over the edge on strange things I've done today. I have to admit it was odd even for me. Debating what to say I start off with something not so stressful "Mother, Sebastian and Jacqueline might come over to go over a few things once the cops leave and they board up the front of the store."

Her once relaxed body went ridged and her eyes popped wide open when she says "COPS, why are they dealing with cops?"

In a soothing voice I say "Calm down, everything is fine. The delivery guy called the cops when he showed up to drop off the food."

Jenny laid her head back down and closed her eyes again. After another few minutes of massaging her feet and legs I was sure she had fallen asleep. I slowly slid out from under her legs and went to the kitchen to check my phone and get a slice of pizza. The instant the box was open I hear Jenny say "Don't eat it all, that's for everybody."

I close the pizza box and check my phone and see there's a message from Mother that says they will be here in fifteen minutes. I head to the couch to wait for everyone else to arrive when I hear a knock on the door. The knock confused me because I wasn't expecting them to be here so quick. I was caught by surprise when I saw Fred standing there holding a frozen dinner so I asked "What's up?"

I could see it bothered him as much as it confused me from his expression of humbleness when he asked "Would there be a way I could use your oven or microwave? The maintenance guy here sucks and hasn't fixed my oven and the microwave is still boxed up."

I laughed slightly and waved for him to come in and said "He really does suck. Sure come on in, just don't disturb Jenny. She's resting on the couch."

He gives me a thumbs up on his way to the kitchen trying to be quiet. I close the door when I hear more footsteps coming up the stairs and open it back up to see Mother and Sebastian stopping in front of my apartment. Once they come in I look back and forth down the hallway to check if it's just the two of them and close the door.

Making my way back to the living room, I find Fred in the fetal position on the kitchen floor as Jenny has the shotgun pointed at him and Sebastian standing over him with his club drawn ready to bash in his head. I rush in between them blocking Fred from any possible blows and say "Stop, stop, stop, he's fine. I told him he could use my oven since I never fixed his."

Jenny walked back to the couch still holding the shotgun at the ready while Sebastian lowered his mace with a defeatist look in his eyes. Fred slowly regained his will to stand and inched his way upright to not alarm anyone with fast movements and says "Shit dude, did you set me up?"

I helped Fred to his feet and said "No, sorry. I forgot to tell them about our arrangement. It's been kinda a busy day."

I avoid looking around the room so I don't have to see the contempt on all of their faces. I could feel six eyes burning through the back of my skull as they wait for an explanation. The ding of the microwave gives me a short moment of relief since Fred knows his cue to leave. Without a word he takes his food and quickly makes his way out of the tense situation. This leaves me alone to answer the question they all want to know but none have asked, what was I thinking?

I turn to face the gallery of my judges and before they could say anything I say "First off, this is my place and I invited him here. B, it's my fault he can't cook on his own because I never fixed the stove. Thirdly, he was a huge help earlier on something I was going to tell all of you. And finally D, he agreed to help us. So if any of you have a problem now is the time to let me know. It was all me and not him."

All at once the three started going off on me to the point that I couldn't tell what was being said by whom. Then as if by some strange power all three voices asked the same thing at the same time making one voice "DO YOU WANT TO DIE?" Then the room fell silent.

The thought of dying never really crossed my mind, but the idea of death didn't phase me the way that it did most. When almost every night as long as I can remember I've seen and lived others deaths. My own mortality was never in question until now. I also never had anyone that wanted me around or relied on me for anything other than to run tests. I could see it in all their eyes how my choices have impacted them. From the fear of losing a love in Jenny's, the anger in Sebastian's that I could bring danger to them, and the despair in Mother's eyes that seemed to hurt me deep and I don't know why.

To do nothing but put a bandage on the situation I say "From now on, I will run everything by you three first, before I do something stupid."

From the doorway I hear Jacqueline say "Make that four of us. I'm not sure what you did now, but I'm part of this as well."

I look at Jacqueline then around to the other three and say "The four of you, is that Okay, are we good now?"

Bowing her head Mother says "We don't want you to question everything you do, we just want you to be careful and think thing through first." The shaking in her voice was hard not to notice and I knew there was something that she knew but didn't want to say, but what was it. She's acted this was towards me since the first day we met in that dark room at the convention.

I knew I had to change the subject so we could move on from this awkward moment in time. Racking my brain to think of a good place to start it came to me so I blurt out "Okay, I know why Akhkharu is stalling." I've never been great with my timing and I knew from the glares I was receiving that this was one of those times.

Mother tries to subtly wipe tears from her eye by turning away and adjusting her blouse and says "Continue with what you were saying."

Jacqueline and Mother join Jenny on the couch, while Sebastian takes the over-sized plush chair near the window where he previously spent days watching the lot across the street. I grabbed a bar stool I had in the kitchen and joined them in the living room where I could face them all.

Now that everyone is situated and somewhat comfortable I begin explaining what I figured out saying "Okay, I know you aren't fans of Fred but I stopped by his place after I left the bookstore the second time. He told me that he wasn't part of any plans just following orders. What Fred did know is that he overheard Akhkharu talking to someone about waiting for me to be at full potential or it's not worth it. So that combined with the stuff I read about him consuming others gifts for his own use, I think if we strike while I'm still a novice he won't actually try to kill me."

Sebastian not know for mixing word says as bluntly as possible "That is the stupidest plan I have ever heard. Are you sure that head injury didn't cause more damage than you told us?"

The others turned to look at him with astonishment, not believing he just said that and Sebastian shrugged his shoulders and said "What? I can't be the only one thinking it." That caused everyone to erupt in laughter.

Once the laughter died down Jenny was the first to speak up saying "So what you're saying is that you go in unprepared and untrained to kill a Sumerian god because you think he only wants your gift if you can be fully trained in a few days. I think Sebastian might be onto something."

Concerned with their faith in me I ask "What do you guys think we should do? I mean, how would it even know if I'm all powered up or not?"

Mother struggling to find the words to describe saying "As your power or gift grows it gives off a sort of feeling to others. It's just an internal awareness that you just know is inside of them. It's hard to explain other than it happening. Your gift is somewhat blocked from detection because of your heritage."

I keep hearing and seeing about my background but nobody has actually explained what it all means so I ask "You and the books say my heritage like I should know what that means, but if I'm so special then why did it land me in a mental hospital and allow me to be tested on for so long. Sorry, that's been weighing on me for a while."

Mother shakes her head knowing she was going to have to do her best to explain not only for them to continue but because Jacob deserves to know the truth says "This isn't going to be easy to say, so please let me explain fully before saying anything." Seeing that this was going to be difficult Jenny got up from the couch and went to stand beside Jacob, wrapping her arm over his shoulder before mother continues "As you probably figured out, the parents that you knew are not your real parents. You were placed with them because they were off the grid and away from those that would want to do you harm while your real parents were away."

I sit in a combination of disbelief and confusion for a few minutes to try and allow what Mother told me to absorb. Jenny pulled me close as I pondered what could be the reason to ditch me as a baby or what was so important that having me around would get in the way.

Before I could say anything Mother says "As for you being in the hospital and being tested on for so long that wasn't by your parents choice. Since you were raised for the first few years off the grid there was no record of your name in the system for them to find you. The hospitals kept what they were doing and your location secret because they knew what they were doing was not only wrong but illegal."

I thought the first load of knowledge was rough but now knowing that I was lost bouncing around the system was basically because of some crooked ass doctors is worse to take in than I could've imagined. The only thing I could think of saying came out "So where are my parents now? You know what it doesn't matter. I don't care, I've made it this far without them. And hey I got you four. We are kinda like family."

Sebastian sitting up from his slouched position says in his ever serious tone "Don't think I'm getting you anything for Christmas or your birthday. You already got my gun."

Jacqueline in a chuckle says "This has got to be the most messed up family of all time, can't wait for the family portrait time."

I know they were trying to lighten the mood and I appreciate it but we have a job to figure out so I don't die horribly or get devoured or whatever that thing wants to do to me. Trying to move on I say "Before we come up with a battle plan we must take care of the most important part first." The four of them looking at me waiting me to say something profound I say "Jenny brought pizza" On that note Sebastian was the first one to the kitchen and digging in as the rest of us followed close behind. Jenny stopped me on the way hugging me tightly. Even though I didn't act like it, she knew I needed it more than I could care to say.

We eat, we joke to keep thing lighthearted for a while trying to make the moment last knowing that the next few days was going to be spent learning, training and planning. As the others went on with their meal I took a second to take a step back and think. This is the single most family like experience that I've had since before I fell from that tree at six. Sure we were a motley crew of misfits. The Wiccan, metal chick, the brute, the wise elder, then you have me the screw up. Hell we even have the fucked up cousin across the hall that nobody wants to talk about. Yep, this is my family.

After our food was gone and we settled into our spots in the living room again, we knew it was time to get to work. Sebastian took a few of the scrolls to see what stands out. Jacqueline started on the Wiccan books to see what she can use for defense. Jenny went over all of our notes that we've made since it all started. Mother took charge of the things in languages that I couldn't figure out, while I went page to page in the book with hidden words. Minute by minute, hour by hour we study every inch of the books and scrolls so nothing was missed. When notes are made they get passed to Jenny to put in her stacks of varying degrees of importance.

The sun went down and back up again and we trudged on taking random breaks for food and hydration. We slept in shifts so no time was wasted. I'm not sure if everything we are doing is wearing on anyone else as much as it me while I read things that aren't actually on the page. The images that I see could very well be my brain turning to mush and not what's on the page at all, but since I'm the only one that can read them there is no way of knowing, so I just make notes of what I see and move on.

When my nap time came around I try to pass it to the next person, but Mother forces me to rest. As I sleep, I get flooded with images and dreams. Too many to make sense of at one time. Things overlapping, an unknown past mixes with a offset present with a dash of several potential futures. These flashes showed me hundreds of deaths with one thing in common, they are all mine.

I'm shaken awake by Sebastian kneeling on the edge of the bed with his massive mitts gripping my shoulders. I must have tossed and turned in my sleep quite a bit because when I tried to get up I was wrapped in the sheet completely immobilized. The sheets seemed damp to the touch from what I assume is sweat but had a tackiness to it. Once coherent Mother turned on the light to better observe my current predicament. I knew something was wrong from the look of fear no Jenny's face as she ran from the room.

Trying to fight my way free from the blankets Sebastian grabbed me tight by the sides and said "Not too fast, we need to remove these slowly so we can check the damage."

The words Sebastian chose, send me into a panic saying " DAMAGE, WHAT DAMAGE?"

Mother trying to be calm I could still hear the worry in her voice as she says "Just relax and let Sebastian get the sheets off of you. It looks like you may have injured yourself while you slept."

With the big man holding me down I don't have a choice but to stay put, so I do everything in my power to calm down. Afraid of how bad it might be I look straight up at the ceiling and focus on the water stains that I've never noticed before. I hear the tearing of the fabric and catch the blade in Sebastian's hand out of the corner of my eye. I know he's good with his weapons so I remain still to make sure he has no reason to slip and split my arm open.

Sebastian gets my attention by snapping his fingers in front of my face. When I adjusted my eyes to see his face he said "Okay, I'm gonna start pulling the blankets away. What I need you to do is stay still until we know what's wrong. Can you do this?" I nod my head yes and lay it back down on the bed.

Mother stepping closer to be near by during the reveal says "Jacob, why don't you close your eyes for now. I'm sure everything is fine but I don't want you going frantic if it's not."

I take a deep breath and close my eyes. I trust them both but I also know that if something is wrong I will still hear it in their voices. Feeling Sebastian's strong left hand take hold of my right shoulder as I notice the blanket being pulled away from my body. As it is slowly stripped back I hear a sound of liquidity suction. The slurping sound continued as I could feel the cold air on my now exposed flesh. No word came from Mother or Sebastian the entire time I was being freed till I the sensation of mobility in my legs then Mother says "Just…. Just let me look you over for a moment before you get up."

I managed to keep my eyes clenched tight knowing it had to be bad with the way she hesitated. "OH DEAR GOD!" I heard Jenny yell from the doorway of the room. This made me jump up from the bed and make a dash to the mirror across the room.

I couldn't believe what I saw in front of me. All the human flesh was gone from my chest and stomach, with only the black hardened new skin exposed and I exclaimed "WHERE THE FUCK IS MY SKIN!"

Mother in an alarmed tone said "It's not just your chest but your entire torso." I spin to see her pointing to the bed where all of my peeled flesh from my back and chest now lay, still stuck to the sheets.

My stomach dropped as I took in the sight of the amount of flesh that was on display. The only thing that came to mind was a snake shedding its old dead outer layer to grow. I return to the mirror to verify what I witnessed on my bed. Scanning my torso, I run my hands over the new black flesh. I seem to have lost all of the human skin from belt line to the base of my neck and from shoulder to shoulder leaving my neck up and arms still appearing normal. The room was silent while I checked over my body until I say "Why... how did this happen?"

Mother walks over to me slowly, looking over my exposed black shell and says "Well.... The only way to really put it is," she pauses to think of the right word before continuing "You are evolving. As you get closer to reaching your potential you are becoming less mortal and more godly."

Eyes wide with horror as I look over my disturbing reflection I ask "Is there any way to stop this, whatever the fuck it is? I mean look at me, I'm more of a freak than before and people wouldn't look at me then."

Sebastian left the room for a few minutes returning with a bucket of soapy water and a few dish rags and set it on the dresser near the mirror. Mother took one of the soapy rags and began cleaning of my back while I did the same to my chest and stomach. As the blood was cleared the my new skin the resemblance of a pliable form of obsidian was more obvious. I heard footsteps coming down the hall stopping just short of the bedroom door. "Is he Okay, can I come in?" Jenny asked trembling, sounding more worried and sad than scared.

Mother took the rag from me and place both of them back into the bucket while Sebastian gathered up the sheets with my old flesh and tossed them in the corner out of sight. The fear of the judgment that jenny might give left me frozen in place. Mother sensing my reluctance went and brought Jenny into the room to show her what had happened saying "He's not hurt so to speak just different in a way."

As Jenny got closer she stretched out her arm reaching to make contact with the new me. As she ran her fingers across my new flesh I felt a shiver run through my body. Her hand retreated back to her chest quickly and said "Did I hurt you?"

I turn to face her and reach out taking her hand into mine softly and pull her to me and say "No babe, it tickled more than anything, which is funny because I've never been ticklish." Jenny gave me a faint smile and relief knowing I was going to be alright set in. That was until her eyes went wide as she looked passed me at something. I was confused of what she saw for a second when I felt something push me forward. There was no sensation on my back other than the push so I turned to see Sebastian with his mace outstretched like he just hit a homerun. I stood in anger at the thought that Sebastian just took a swing at me. I can only assume that Mother pushed me out of the way before impact. I looked for mother to confirm my suspicion that she had been the one to save me but realized there was no way she could push me from behind at her distance from me.

Sebastian dropped his bone club and backed away from me finding himself stuck in the corner with nowhere to go. He raised his hands in a defensive stance afraid of what might happen saying "I'm sorry, I don't know what made me do that."

Confused of why he was so afraid, I've never seen him scared of anything. He always faced a fight with a smile from my experience with him. I picked up his weapon and walked towards him with it out for him to take saying "Dude, it's cool. You didn't even get me. Somehow I moved out of the way."

Sebastian took the club from me skittishly and said "That's the thing, I didn't miss. I hit square in your back as hard as I could swing it."

I look at Jenny and Mother for confirmation. Mother shakes her head yes and Jenny still startled did the same. Mother stepped near me and turning me so she could inspect my back for any marks and running her hand down my back says "there's nothing here, tell me when you feel something." I shake my head in acknowledgment and wait.

Standing still preparing for Mother to do something to my back when I feel that same tingle from earlier and I say "There…. Right there, I can feel that. What is it?"

I turned to see Jenny raising her hand and she says "That was me, I ran my hand down your back. You didn't feel anything else?"

I shook my head no and said "No, why? What else did you try?" I look down at mother's hand and see her hold Sebastian's knife that he used to cut the sheets away from me and I say "You're messing with me right, you didn't actually try cutting me with that thing did you?"

Mother smiled a guilty smile and said "Yes I did and not a scratch"

I look over at Sebastian and he is still standing in the corner with an even more concerned look on his face than I had and I say "Sebastian, come on out of the corner. It's cool. Let's all go to the living room, it's starting to smell in here." On our way out of the room I grab a shirt and put it on so everyone stops staring at me. As I walk into the living room I say "Okay, real quick before we get back to planning. Please, and I stress please don't try to stab or hit me with anything else for now. I already feel odd enough."

Everyone agrees and settles in for more research and planning, Sebastian even relaxes around me again. It still concerns me what he said about not wanting to hit me but he had to. What could that mean? Did something take control of his body or was he just following Mother's order. There's no time to use in dwelling on it now, we have to move forward and get ready for the upcoming battle that could turn into an all out war in a heartbeat. There were questions that still needed answered on so many aspects of this entire ordeal but the time was slipping away.

Jenny sat next to me, as we went through the flesh book. She was writing, as I was looking for something of note to pop out at me when a thought came to her.

"What do all these books have in common with each other?" she blurts out. Not sure where she was going with we all sat in silence wondering if it was a rhetorical question when she says "They are all from different time periods and tell different parts of the history as Akhkharu progressed."

Mother understood where Jenny was going with this and says "Yes, we just need to put them in order and it will be a timeline of events. To finish this timeline we should bring that Fred guy over here for a little recent history."

Sebastian started getting up from his chair and I stopped him saying "Go ahead and stay here big man, I think you still scare him too much."

Sebastian sat back down as I headed for the door and said "Fine, you get him. It's not my fault he takes a hit like a bitch." I think not hurting me took something out of the big man. It was a shock to us all I'm guessing. He's use to brute for working and it didn't even phase me.

Standing in front of Fred's door I knock hard hoping he's home when an unknown voice yells "WHO IS IT AND WHAT DO YOU WANT?"
Trying to protect him from his Master's wrath if this person would find out he was helping us I say "Sorry to bother you, but it's maintenance. I got a work order for this apartment. Is there a Frederick here, and can I speak to him please?" I listen closely for any movement on the other side of the door with no luck.

The voice says in an irritated tone "He's not here, you are going to have to come back later."

Thinking to myself that he could be at work and just have a friend staying over to help him unpack his stuff I say "Okay, thanks could you please be sure to let him know I came by to fix the stove and I can come back tomorrow if that works for him."

"Sure will" the voice says in a somewhat creepy way "But I'm sure you will have a lot on your plate tomorrow to worry about the stove." The voice said closer than before then started laughing as if it knew me and what was going down soon.

I back up slowly and go back into my apartment locking the door behind me. I stood on my side of the door looking through the peephole quietly hoping to catch a glimpse of whomever that voice belonged to.

Jenny saw me staring out and came up behind me and says "Whatcha lookin at babe?" as she wraps her arms around my waist from behind me.

Without taking my eye off the peep hole in fear of missing something I say "Nothing, maybe something. Oh who the hell knows." Turning back to face her keeping her arms around my waist I kiss her on the lips and say "I'll tell everyone in a sec, I'm probably over thinking things." And we head back to the couch.

I retell the events that just happened of my failed retrieval attempt of Fred and the looks I received caused me to worry more than I was moments earlier. Jacqueline was pacing the room nervously stopped to say "So basically, we could all be trapped right now."

Mother turns to her and says "Possibly, but we won't know unless one of us tries to leave."

Sebastian postures in his chair and says "I'll try, and if they try to stop me I will crush them like the last batch." Everyone looks from side to side to get a read on how this sounded when he got to his feet and started for the door.

I hurry towards him and stop him from leaving and say "Give me a sec to get my boots on and load the shotgun just in case you need help." I slip my boots on and grab the gun and shells and start reloading when I hear the door close behind him. From the hallway I hear a smash on my door and watch the door handle fall to the floor. Then the sound of Sebastian's heavy footsteps moving quickly down the rear stairwell followed by several other sets of footsteps moving faster towards his. Mother, jenny and I try to jimmy the door open franticly to go help or at least warn him of his pursuers with no luck. I turn to Jacqueline and shout "SHOTGUN, BRING ME·MY SHOTGUN!!!" Within seconds she tossed it down the hallway to me. Mother and Jenny moved out of the way as I took aim. The echo of the shot in this small area caused our ears to ring. Not letting the discomfort slow me down I reached through the hole and yanked the door open only to find I had put a hole through a waiting attacker who lay dead. His fluids coated the wall where he now rests.

I turn towards Mother and Jenny and say "Get something, anything to defend yourselves and get in a room and lock it until I come back."

As I turn to leave I see my tool belt on the floor. I grab my short handled sledge from its pouch and hand Jenny my shotgun. I take off down the hall and dart down the rear stairwell, clearing two even three stairs at a time until I reached the bottom. Throwing my shoulder into the exit door it flew open breaking the spring hinge.

Once in the back lot I feverishly looked around for any sign of Sebastian or his attackers. From the way the dirt was kicked up and the dust still in the air there was clearly a scuffle but not one body in sight.

As I let the dust settle I listen. The only sound in the air is the traffic in the distance, no screams, no running footsteps on the concrete, not ever the smashing from a brawl. Now that the air has cleared I see blood splatter littering the side of the dumpster like graphite. The amount of blood had to come from someone, and that someone would still be draining out leaving a trail to follow. I follow the crimson trail to the street where it stops. Maybe there was a car waiting, maybe they took some poor bastards car that was driving by at the wrong time.

Standing in the road lost, I hear a scream followed by the loud boom of a shotgun. Snapped back to reality, oh no Jenny. Running as fast as I could move my legs I make it through the back door. Unable to judge my distance as my eyes adjusted to the dark hallway I missed the first step, causing myself to collided face first onto the stairwell. Scrambling to my feet I used the sledge hammer to hook the railing and propel forward. As I worked my way up the what seemed like endless flights of stairs there were two more blasts of the shotgun.

As I made it to my floor I noticed another body laying in a gutted mess. Not knowing what awaits inside my apartment, I charge head first without delay. Checking each room as I make my way down the hallway and I yell "JENNY, MOTHER, JACQUELINE, ANYONE!!!"

The sounds of scuffling in the living room caught my ear while I was in the bedroom. I hurry to help with my hammer ready to attack. I find Jacqueline laying on the floor with Fred sprawled on top of her, neither one was moving. I look up to see Mother standing with her back to the wall with two shotgun shells in her mouth as she reloads the weapon. Jenny is kneeling next to her with her arm outstretched and appears in pain gripping her temple with her right hand. My eyes follow the direction she is reaching to see one of the goons suspended to the corner where the ceiling meets the wall. When she notices I'm in the room her arm drops and the man falls to the floor. Without hesitation I charge the thug ready to crush his skull. He springs to his feet, with his knife drawn then boom. The blast of the shotgun levels the assailant, exploding his right rib cage. The concussion pounded my eardrums causing me to lose balance and drop to my knees.

Through the ringing in my ears I hear one of the women ask if that was all of them. Shaking my head in an effort to regain my bearings I feel a touch on my left shoulder. Turning to see who was next to me I see Jenny. She helped me to my feet as the ringing subsides, I grab her and hold her tightly. With a clear head I remember Jacqueline and Fred on the floor. Jenny helps me over to help Mother with Jacqueline, she was carefully rolling Fred to the side off of her. Looking at the two laying there I say "Well I guess we know what side he was on. Kinda thought we might be able to trust him."

Jenny pushes me out of the way to check on Fred for a pulse and see if he's breathing and says "Actually he tackled Jacqueline to save her from being bashed with a club and got himself hit instead." Amazed of what I was just told I help her lay him out flat and then do the same for Jacqueline.

While we waited for them to come around I explained what I saw outside. Mother assured me that Sebastian could take care of himself and I knew he could but something didn't seem right about it. This entire situation was wrong. Why attack now, why here? Nothing was adding up. With the meeting tomorrow the only thing that worked to Akhkharu's favor was us not knowing where Sebastian was. They lost more men, raising the body count too high to remember.

I sit back against the wall and look around at the massacre in my apartment. The realization hit me that I was going to lose the only place I've been able to call my own and home. The furniture that I've collected over time from when people either move and no longer want or someone dying and the family didn't feel like hauling away. There wasn't a single piece item that didn't get broke or decorated in blood. You can't forget the fist size holes in the walls and my front door. The worry set in of what might have happened to Sebastian. I know he's tough but who knows what they brought to the party.

The only comfort I have is that Mother and Jenny were safe and Jacqueline seems to have just been knocked out. Fred could even make it. I get off the floor and walk over to the closest dead body. Leaning down I grab it by it's feet and begin dragging it to the kitchen linoleum floor to make it easy to clean up the blood pools when there's a knock on the door and I hear the meek little voice of the elderly woman from 4E, the Widow Hess saying "Hello, hello dear. Jacob are you home?"

Dropping the dead guys legs I hurried to the door before she came in and the nice old lady has a heart attack on me. Pretty sure calling 911 would be bad news with the amount of blood spilled. I catch the door as it starts to swing open and come face to face with Miss Hess and I say "Hey there ma'am, how can I help you?"

Startled from me appearing in the doorway so sudden she took a step back and said "I was watching my stories and there was a few big banging sounds, is everything Okay?"

I step out into the hallway and start walking her back up to her floor and I remember Tim telling me that she was hard of hearing and was mostly blind from her cataracts so I say "Everything's fine, I'm just doing some remodeling to get ready for new people to move in. Soon we will have this place full again."

We arrive at her door and Miss Hess says "Oh, that will be nice, hopefully they are some nice elderly people. Not like the last ones that moved in. If they are you can shoot them as well, like those two that were in the hallway down there."

Caught off guard by her response I say "What do you mean?"

She smiles saying "I'm old child, not stupid. It's okay, I'm sure you had good reasons. Mother said there would come a time." She shut the door leaving me speechless and confused and thinking if Mother knows everybody.

Heading back to my apartment to so I can continue my clean up. Walking in is see Jacqueline had awaken and moved to the couch while Fred sat up and was rubbing a rather large knot on the back of his head.

Mother is sitting near Jacqueline talking to her quietly while Jenny is coming out of the kitchen with two bags of ice. She handed one to Jacqueline on her way by and tossed the other to Fred. He reaches up when I get close and I take his hand pulling him to his feet. Helping him steady himself I say "So I hear you were kind of a hero."

As he holds the ice pack on the back of if head he says "I don't really feel like one. What the hell did I get hit with anyways?" Taking the pack off his head I check out the golf ball sized lump on his head.

I move his hand with the ice pack back to the lump and say "No clue, but whatever the hell it was it left a mark. I would keep that on there for a while. Thanks for the assist."

Fred makes his way through the carnage to the over-sized chair and brushes off the plaster fragments and sits down and says "It's no problem, I couldn't let them hurt the women."

I tip one of the kitchen chairs back upright, moving it close to the couch where Jenny now sat and sit down slowly not knowing how sturdy it is when the front door is kicked open. I grab the shotgun aiming down the hall and see Sebastian standing there with tattered close and drenched in blood and filth. As Sebastian walks towards us with labored steps he says in the angriest tone ever spoken "They hit me with a fucking car." When he saw Fred sitting in his chair across the room his steps became faster and more deliberate. He produced his bone mace from behind his back. The weapon was dripping with blood and only he knows what.

Mother saw where he was going and got in between him and his injured target saying "Hold it right there." Putting a hand on his chest. "He is fine to be here, he saved Jacqueline's life. He took the blow so she was safe. So you just sit down and tell us what happened and where you've been."

Sebastian begrudgingly backed down saying "Fine, he can stay. But not in my chair, MOVE." Fred didn't hesitate quickly getting out up from the chair and moved around the couch out of reach of the big man to find a new place to sit.

Sebastian not waiting for Fred to find a spot says "well, this is what happened. As I went down the stairs I heard them behind me on the stairs. When I got out the door I stepped to the side and waited for the first one to come out and I swung, crushing his ribs. Someone shocked me with a stun gun from behind. So I threw an elbow back hitting him in the jaw. I moved to the more open part of the lot so I could get full swings when one of those sons of bitches ran into me with a car. Then like eight of them drug me into the back seat and speed off. When I got my hands free I just started swinging at anything and everything. I guess I hit the driver causing him to wreck. Now I'm here."

Mother reached forward and patted Sebastian on the knee and says "I'm glad you are back and safe." He sat quietly but I could tell that Sebastian was still fueled by anger and couldn't wait to dish out a whole mess of payback.

The silence in the room after the feverish attack was unnerving to me so I blurt out "Jenny has super powers." Everyone in the room looked at me, most with astonishment but some with horror that I said that. Their eyes one by one left me and drifted to Jenny.

Jenny lowered her head appearing ashamed of what she did and said "I don't know what I did. He came at me and I reacted. That's never happened before."

I pull her close and as she resisted slightly to let me know I shouldn't have brought it up. As I held her I say "It will be okay sweetheart. You can shoot magic out of your hands and I have weird black bullet proof skin and I can hitchhike in dreams. We are perfect together, like the less than dynamic duo." She smiled and pushes me.

Fred who's been quiet for a while adjusted in his chair and says "Worst superheroes ever." The laughter erupts for a moment till the pains of our recent interaction remind us how banged up we were. Reality is a cruel beast at times, not allowing you a moment to rest and get your head straight before piling the more on to attempt to bury you alive.

A little levity is a welcome release every now and then but I know what what's coming up I need to prepare. Trying to work our way through the mounds of research to find the most recent information has proven to be a daunting task. We've read every book, scroll and note so many time we can almost recite them word for word then I hits, Fred. Some of this might stand out to his fresh eyes.

In my own special way of coming up with bad ideas and acting on them I decide to act the others "Don't kill me for saying this but I have an idea. What if we let Fred check over stuff and see if any light bulbs come on? I mean he has spent time around and following this thing."

From the looks on everyone's faces you would think I just spoken mandarin, but after a short time of discussing it quietly amongst themselves Mother says "Another perspective could be useful. Something here might be similar to something he has read while he was with them."

Sebastian with less attitude now towards Fred, tosses him a large, thick book and says "Fine with me, but remember this is your idea and I will skin him alive if he screws us over." Thinking it was over, we all get back to work when Sebastian finishes his statement "And make you hold him while I do it."

I shake my head knowing that he means what he says and that it's not a scare tactics and say "Such anger, you need a hobby. You know something to help you get that aggression out in a constructive way."

We were all back in research mode when Sebastian without looking up from his scroll says "I like needle point." This caused me to lose my place in the book and look up at him.

Mother shook her head yes and says "It's true, he's really good at it." Pulling off her scarf and tossing it to me she says "He made me this."

I looked at the intricate design work that was stitched on the scarf. Passed it to Jenny so she could see doing my damnedest not to crack up. I can only guess Sebastian could see my smirk and while my head was down he lobbed a piece of the broken table at my head. I dodged it just in time to have it clear my right ear by a fraction of an inch. Knowing Mother was probably giving one of her disapproving glares I opened my book and continued reading.

I hear Sebastian mumbling something to himself so I say "Sorry, big man. You do good work. Better than I could do, hell I can't even saw on a button."

Fred chuckled and says "Who doesn't know how to sew on a button?"

Thinking about it I look at him and say "Well, the doctors didn't let me have sharp objects in the loony bin and when I got out I never really tried to do it. I'm pretty sure I don't own any clothes with buttons."

Fred continues scanning the notes that Jenny had gotten in order and says "Weirdo." I get ready to respond and he sits up fast and says "I think I found something, here help me clear a spot to lay these out." Jenny and I push the broken table out of the way and push the books into a pile.

Fred , taking the notes takes a knee on the floor. He tears the pages from the notebook as he lays them on the floor in an order only he knows. Once everything is where he wants it he sits back on his heel and says "I can't believe nobody caught it before now."

Looking at the what appeared random pages that were laid out Jacqueline says "Catch what? I'm afraid you might need to explain what you are talking about."

Fred seemed excited as he crawled to the other side of the pages so he could explain. He started at the first page in his top row and says "It's a cycle. Every entry or documented time Akhkharu showed up coincides with the eclipse. He needs the time without abilities to prepare himself to take a new one. At that point he disappears for a while to learn how to use it."

Jenny scooted closer to the pages and says "How did you get that from the notes? No offense but we've been looking these for days."

Fred confident in his theory continues his explanation "It's all right here." Pointing from page to page "Each time he shows up he's stronger and can do something new that wasn't in the last book. Which means..."
Jenny stepped in and finished his sentence saying "Which means he only comes out of hiding to take an ability that is needed for whatever his endgame Is."

As I let the new information settle in my brain I lean back in my chair and ask the question "So what is his endgame?"

Mothers tone was of concern when she says "Of course, it's to take revenge against Tiamat for casting him out."

Not thinking before I spoke I say "Well does anyone know how to get hold of this Tiamat? According to the lore she's some sort of giant dragon. I don't think it would be that hard to track down something like that."

Mother shifts in her seat not knowing how to reply eventually says "That might prove more difficult than you would think. If you believe the stories Tiamat was killed in a war with Marduk. Marduk created heaven and hell from the two halves of her body. But there is a story that said she vowed to return one day and regain her throne with the help of the humans she gifted."

Jenny sat back down saying "Oh well, I guess we can scratch calling the Mother of all creation for help off of the list of people to recruit."

Clapping my hands together I say "I guess we need to come up with a plan of attack." I point to Fred "I assume tomorrow is just one big trap designed to make me think without his abilities he is helpless. Am I correct."

Fred gathers up the papers in the new order and says "Unfortunately, you are correct. But on a good note, you did kill over half of the followers I know of. So yay for that."

I hold up my hand to Sebastian for a high five only to be left hanging. So I lower my hand and say "See, we knew what we were doing…. Sort of." Jenny smacked me in the back of the head knowing that one of the people that hurt was sitting in the room with us and is on our side now.

Going in knowing it's a trap changed the game but the trick will be to have that change be in our favor. We eat and we plan, with each plan being more outlandish than the next. They range from the completely idiotic to the extremely dangerous and I know what part of the spectrum mine fell on. The others decided to nap in their spot, all except for Sebastian and I. Sebastian stood staring out the window watching the house where it all started.

It's not that I couldn't sleep but it was more that I didn't want to knowing what happened the last time. I grabbed my phone and started watching videos on the internet. I came across one that stood out to me as something that could work or ever give me a slight distraction. Keeping the idea to myself I did a little more searching on how to set up my new plan and a few clicks later it was done.

Jenny leaned over on me and woke up when the light on my phone shined in her face. She tries focusing her eye and says "What's up, what are you doing?"

Hoping she didn't see what I was up to I close my screen and set my phone on the floor and say "can't sleep, so I'm playing on the internet."

She shifts a little and says "You need your rest babe. Tomorrow is going to be bad enough to add being dead ass tired on top of it."

I kiss her forehead and snuggle closer to her feeling that I might have finally had a good idea and say "You're right babe, let's get some rest. It's going to be a long day."

I'm awaken by the smell of biscuits, gravy and gravity, mostly it was the gravity. Jenny had gotten up and I fell smacking my face on the wall next to me. Once I peel my face off the wall I looked around and noticed everyone was eating but me. After I crawled myself to my feet, I made my way to the kitchen where I find a plate waiting for me. I dig in before leaving the kitchen and ate while I walk back to my chair.

The room is a mixture of somber, anxious and worried anticipation. We eat our food in silence, which seemed to make the tension worse. When I finished my food I took the plate to the kitchen and headed to my bedroom to grab the heavy leather jacket that Sebastian gave me to use on the first interaction with Akhkharu.

When I get to the living room, I take Jenny's plate and hand her the jacket and say "Sebastian gave me this to protect me when I went to save you that first time. Now it will protect you, try it on." She holds up the jacket, eyeing the immense size and questioning my logic. "Trust me, it will fit. Don't ask me how, but it will." Sebastian gave me a look of approval as did Mother.

Jenny took off her hoodie and slide the jacket on. Once zipped the jacket shrank to be form fitting, Jenny's eyed widened as it adjusted and says "This is awesome, it fits perfectly." She put her hoodie back on over top of the leather jacket and looked at her reflection in the mirror. "You can't even tell I'm wearing it."

I walk over to her as she admires herself and I say "If you think that's cool, check this out." Taking her fork off of the plate I was holding I stab her in the shoulder.

She flinched upon impact and turned to swing when I held up the fork showing her that the prongs were bent and it didn't actually go through the jacket. The anger in her eyes was evident when she says "That freaking hurt, you dick." As I reached to tell her I was sorry, she kicks me right in the knee, sending me to tumbling to the floor.

Sure I was over playing the kick but I did feel shitty for not thinking through the whole stabbing her with a fork thing. I wanted her to feel like she got in a good shot meanwhile Sebastian is laughing so hard I'm afraid he might forget to breathe. The tension lifted and spirits raised for the briefest of moments and I knew I was at least good for the comic relief.

After I returned standing I walked up behind Jenny and wrapped my arms around her waist and whispered in her ear "I'm sorry babe. I don't think at times. All I want to do is keep you safe."

She turned to face me, still in my arms and said "Well not stabbing me is a good place to start." Jenny kissed me and then we let go of each other. She went and grabbed the notebook that had our detailed plans of the upcoming evening's events and began flipping through.

Jenny stands looking around the room at the rest of us and says "Okay, let's make sure we all on the same page. When I point to you say your part of the plan." As she scanned the room her finger eventually landed on Jacqueline.

Jacqueline sat up and grabbed her notes and says "We can already assume that they are setting up themselves, so I from a distance will charge the wards that I put in place before I came over. They've been sitting dormant until I cast the spell. This should keep them at bay for a short time."

Jenny glances at Sebastian and gave him the nod. He picks up his mace and says "Well I'm going to be ready in the stairwell out of sight until those insects decide to show their faces. That's when I get to have some fun." The smile grew on his face as he thought of the retribution that he will be able to receive.

Jenny pointed at Fred who was surprised to be called on next. A little nervous he says "Ummm, I'm going to hope that they still think I'm on their side and get as close to them as I can and take them out one by one. When I get that part done I'm going to use this charm thing to get closer to Akhkharu to make it look like I'm helping him and provide Jacob with backup or distraction. Providing I don't die before that."

I look at Fred and give him a thumbs up and quietly say "Don't worry, we got your back."

Before Jenny could call on the next person Mother started talking "My part is going to be hard to explain. I'm going to try to get inside our advisories heads to try to control them or plant at least a seed of doubt in their minds enough to sway them from getting in the way. That is until the eclipse happens and all gifts are lost."

That last part concerned me so I ask Mother "With the gifts going away for a short time how will that effect my skin? I mean it's not exactly an ability but a part of me."

Mother seemed stumped by my question for a second and then says "I'm not really sure, I assume that it being part of you it will remain the same as it is, but not being to sure I would prefer you stay a safe distance anyway. Even without his abilities, if he is the way you described those claws could be deadly."

Jenny checking things off on the notes looks up and says "Since my newly discovered ability has only been used once, I don't plan on trying it out with everything going to be on the fritz. That leaves me staying back and protecting Mother as she's in the zone with no way to know what's going on around her. Fred is it still cool that we use your place since the door still has the ability to lock and close?" Fred gave her a thumbs up and tosses Jenny the key to his apartment.

All eyes were now on me. I stood up and started pacing the floor. Knowing the entire plan as a whole was just to protect me I got nervous. I say "First part I'm to gear up and load the shotgun and make sure it's working properly. Next I'm going to need to be down there and ready to go in something like five and a half hours or something."
Sebastian interrupts me and says "Five hours forty two minutes."

Still pacing I point to Sebastian and continue from where I was "Thanks. Five hours and forty ones minutes now. Then I meet up with big ugly and try not to die. Also I need to kill him dead and dismember his body making sure the pieces stay apart for good or he could come back. I hope it works because I'm not completely sure I read that part right. One more thing." I grab my phone and toss it to Jenny and say "Don't worry about why right now, but when you see me approach Akhkharu hit send on the message. It's already on the screen."

Jenny looks at the phone confused not knowing what to think and says "What did you do? Remember you were going to run all of your stupid ideas by us first."

To reassure her I walk over and run my hands up and down her arms and say "I know, I know but this isn't one of my half cocked plans. It's just something to draw attention away from all of us and by time for me to get in closer."

Jenny puts the phone in her pocket shaking her head in frustration. Sebastian got up and went to the kitchen and opens the refrigerator, leaning over and looking from shelf to shelf says "You know you are a dumbass right, and you're probably going to get us all killed?"

All I could do is laugh, they haven't even heard the plan and already have us doomed to perish violently. On that note Fred got up and started for the door. I jog after him and say "Wait up, where you going? We still got a few hours to kill, you know before the killing. Sorry that came out wrong."

Fred stops and turns and says "I got a few things to take care of before the end of the world happens. That and if I'm planning on blending in with them I should probably go and be there to see what they have planned and what they want me to do."

I pat him on the back and say "Good thinking, good luck with that and try not to die." Fred heads out the door and I can hear his footsteps head down the front steps. Turning back to the others I see everyone gathering up what they need for their part of the plan. Sebastian is wiping down his bone mace, Mother sitting on the couch doing breathing exercises with her eyes closed to focus her mind.

I notice Jacqueline digging through a large bag that she brought occasionally pulling out small glass bottles with what looks like different herbs inside. My curiosity peaked I go grab my chair and set it down close to her and sit. I ask Jacqueline "What do you got going on over here?"

She sets a few of them out in front of her and points to them one at a time saying "Each one has a different purpose. This is sage, it's to help clear the air of the bad. This is.."

I stop her and say "Never mind, I will probably forget anyway. I will leave you be to do your magic hocus-pocus stuff. With my luck I will more than likely blow us all up or something." From the way she gently took the bottle back from me that I didn't remember picking up she knows I'm right on thinking that.

I look around the room for Jenny and see her leaning against the wall next to the couch, head down with her earbuds in. Her head slowly bobbing to the music. Careful not to startle her I use my foot to tap the heel of her boot. When she looked up at me she removed one of her ear buds so she can hear me say "Come with me, I got something to show you." I reach down and she takes my hand, pulling herself to her feet.

I lead her out of the apartment and down the hall. We come to a set of stairs that are blocked with a do not enter sign on a rope. I take the rope down and take her hand having her follow me up the stairs towards a dark doorway. The lights have never worked in this part of the building and none of the electricians that have been hired could figure out why. I jiggle the handle on the door a few time and it opens. I lead her into the dark attic and we stand still for and I dig through my pocket for a lighter. I strike the lighter and say "Wait here for just a sec." I go to the corner and find the candles that I had up left up here and light it. With the glow of the candle I search for the other candles, lighting them one at a time till the room brightens up. The dancing of the flames allows me to see the worry and fear in her eyes.

I pull a stool over to Jenny, and dust it off so she had a place to sit and I close the door to the room so I know we aren't going to be disturbed. Once the door is closed the stills and the flames find their home and remain stationary. I take a seat in front of her on a stack of old filter pads with a ratty blanket draped across it. I see her trying to look around the room and taking it in one section at a time. With confusion in her voice she asks "What is this place?"

I hold out my arms to the side and in an ashamed tone I say "This use to be home." I could see she didn't have a clue what I was talking about so I say "When I was released on my own for the first time I use to squat here. I would sneak in and sleep up here when it was cold out. The owner found me one day and offered me a job and a place to stay instead of calling the cops. I guess he took pity on me due to my appearance."

The tears welled up in Jenny's eyes, despite her attempt to hold them in. Using my sleeve I reach up and wipe the tears away and she says "I had no idea."

I scoot in closer and say "It's okay, nobody knew. I kind of keep this part of my life private. There's a lot that I don't tell anyone. And as of late there's a lot I don't even know about myself."

Jenny trying her best to keep the water works from flowing sniffles and says "Well you got me and the others now. You can tell me anything and I won't judge you, you know that right."

I shake my head yes and say "I know I do, that's why I'm showing you now. We have no way of knowing what's going to happen later. I just come up here every now and again to remember where I started. It was a simpler time, nobody trying to kill me."

She laughed a little as she dried her eyes saying "I know what you mean. How am I expected to deliver dumbasses food with what I know now. Never knowing what lurks behind the next door."

Seeing her smile helped me relax and I say "You could always be like me and charge in blindly without a worry in the world. Well actually I do have worries, you and the others. I forgot what it was like to have people that care about you."

Jenny leaned down from the stool taking my face in her trembling hands, pulling me forward and kissed my forehead. Her touch sends an electricity through my body that the longer she held on the more amped I became. I reach out with both hands and pull her down to the makeshift bed with me. As we kissed the power built causing sparks to shoot off in every direction. I could what looks like lightning in her eyes.

Our connection grew as we became more entangled and intertwined. Clothing quickly is shed leaving us exposed. The bolts bounce between us and spanked around the room as she rode me giving the appearance of a human Tesla coil.
As our sweat drips, it sizzles on contact with any other surface but our bare flesh. My once onyx like new skin now seems glow a bright electric blue. The passion intensifies, sending pulses of lightning under my remaining human flesh. Nothing could stop the light show that was us.

My mortal exterior smokes from the power that is being conducted through my demigod form. Jenny has sparks coming off her fingertips and her body is starting to be consumed by a blinding blue flame. Her moans crackle, the flame around her overtook us both, and causing our combined figures to hover higher and higher.

Together we climax with a shockwave basting from our limp bodies, sending us crashing to the floor. As we separate, I lay on the floor staring at the ceiling in the attic both exhausted and charged. Jenny rolled to my side and I wrap my arm around her. She ran her finger across my chest. I could feel the sparks snapping as she made contact, she says "How long do you think your skin will keep glowing? Just wondering because I think it would be kinda awkward every time we do something you have to walk around like a bug light."
I roll to my side to face her and notice that my arms were glowing like my chest and vacant of mortal flesh. I look over the rest of my body and see that every inch of my naked flesh was the same as my chest and arms. Slightly afraid of what I might find I reach for my face. Running my hand across my cheek I feel the familiar scar skin I knew.

Now on my feet standing naked in the middle of the room with the pulsing blue glow radiating like an old neon sign. I look down and see Jenny laying on her back smiling up at me. I knelt down as she sat up. I take her hand and kiss it softly and say "I love you. I'm not going anywhere."

Smiling she says "That's good, because you're stuck with me now. After what we just did you think I'm going to let you get away." Jenny reached for her clothes and pulled her phone out of her pocket and checking the time. "Oh shit!" she exclaimed "We've been up here for over four hours. Get dressed." She says as she tosses my pants at me. "We got to get back to the others.

We threw our clothes on as fast as we could move. There wasn't any time to waste the deadline was only an hour away. Blowing out the last lit candle. The room had a faint glow that was coming from under my clothes. We made our way back down stairs to my apartment rushing inside to find the other three standing in the living room talking.

We walk in to join them and I say "Sorry, sorry, we lost track of time."

Sebastian looks us over and says "Where the hell have you been? What could be so important that you want to cost the entire mission?"

Mother notices the glow coming through my shirt. It was faint in the light but still noticeable and says "I know where they've been and it's none of our business. All that matters is they're back now." The smile mother has made Jenny blush and look away.

I check the clock on the wall and realize there's only forty-five minutes before go time. I grab my shotgun off the table and dump my satchel out on the floor. I find the box of ammo and load up my pockets. Once I get all the rounds I can fit I load the shotgun. Loaded and ready to go I say "Alright everyone, let's get to it."

Jenny dug through her pockets finding Fred's keys and grabs Mothers bag so they could make their way across the hall. Jacqueline picks up her bag of herbs and follows them to the door. Right before they make it to the door Jenny runs back over and kisses me and says "One for good luck, remember you promised me you would come back."

I smile and say "I know and I will. You know you never told me you loved me back."

Jenny turned and headed to the door and says "I will when you come back." Then she was gone into Fred's apartment.

Sebastian and I stand silent and alone in the room. The last time I remember we were alone he was leading me down a dark hallway the first time we met. Time counting down to the main event all we could do is stare blankly at each other not knowing what to say. Sebastian looked uneasy in our silence says "I'm going to go." And he started for the door. As he crossed the threshold he hollered back "Oh yeah, don't fuck up and die. It will crush Mother"

I stood there shaking my head in amazement at his bluntness I yell back "yeah, good luck to you too." Now alone, and time no longer on my side, I don't know what to do with the remaining half hour.

I stand practicing my quick draw of the shotgun from under my jacket in front of the mirror for a few minutes. Getting impatient I head to the window in the living room and take a look at the meeting place and notice the house is fading. This once solid building that I was in is not nothing more than a misty figure. I look up at the sky and see the eclipse is fast approaching.

Zipping up my jacket I make my way out of my apartment stopping to take possibly my last look. Saying my goodbyes to everyone quietly to all of them to myself as I walked down the front stairwell and out the front door. Bracing myself for what may happen in the next ten minutes I take a deep breath and push the door open.

The first step outside I can feel the warmth of the sun on my face. As I get closer to the curb I see a shrouded figure emerging from the mist-like house. I can only assume it's Akhkharu, but he isn't as big as I remember from our last encounter.

The figure approaches slowly and I see the shrouded head turn back and forth. I can only assume it's searching over the area. The dark opening of the creatures hood settles on my location. Even though I'm more than a little freaked out on what could go down, I stand calmly leaning against the light post with my hands in my jacket pockets. Faking like I know what I'm doing is a specialty of mine. That's probably the only reason I haven't been fired from my current job yet.

The eclipse begins, darkening the sky. The once bright sun is becoming dim as the moon takes it's place. The figure steps forward and begins to pull the shroud off it's head. I when the light hits the exposed flesh on its right hand I see the scales of the dragon-like claw. As the hood dropped and the robe removed Akhkharu grew in size to take the form of the beast that I remember.

Carefully shifting my hand inside my jacket pocket I find the grip for my shotgun. The hole I cut in the lining gave me better access to the trigger. Taking a few steps into the street I do my best to hide the nerves in my voice when I say "Looks like I figured out your little riddle, are you surprised?"

Now free of his garments Akhkharu stretched and flexed his massive patchwork frame and in his thick accent says "I was a bit worried for a moment but I knew you would find a way. Come closer and let me look at you."

I take a look up to check on how much time I had before the eclipse was in full effect. It seems to be happening faster and faster. I'm sure he wants me within reach so he can snatch me up for his pre eclipse snack but I would rather not become trail mix if I can do anything about it so holding my ground I say "No thanks, I'm good right where I'm at for the time being. Maybe in a few minutes."

Kicking his robes out of the way Akhkharu says "Don't worry boy, I'm not here to hurt you. This is just a meeting."

Taking a half step a step closer to him I say "You know, that's what my proctologist said to me before and that turned out to be a pain in the ass." From the heaving of his chest and snarling lips I knew I was getting to Akhkharu and I had him right where I wanted his big freaky ass. If I take a few more steps my plan will go into effect. That is if Jenny remembers to hit send.

The sun is now consumed by the moon leaving only the ring of fire visible. I take my final two steps closer to Akhkharu, landing just out of lunging reach of those razor sharp talons. I guess he was waiting for the same thing because I see no less than a dozen of his little acolytes filing onto the street and from behind the house. Fred was there and took his place at the left hand of the beast.

In what seemed an eternity of our Mexican standoff no one made a move. Just as I took a hesitant step forward I heard my saving grace, my plan was happening. The sound of two dozen stereos kicked on at once all blasting MJ's Thriller followed by forty choreographed dancers hit the street all painted up like zombies. The actors surrounded me making it easy to slip away from sight and make my way around the back of the acolytes unnoticed.

In the confusion Akhkharu became restless and orders "FIND HIM, BRING HIM TO ME!!!"

The minions rushed to follow their masters orders in fear of repercussions. Charging head first into the crowd. From my vantage point I see the bodies of the acolytes fly into the air one at a time. My only guess is they found the business end of Sebastian's be good stick. One by one our odds increased as the bodies dropped. The actors scattered in all directions but toward Akhkharu. Fred had stayed put at the masters left side. I not sure if it is to help us or serve him but the time for testing his loyalty is next.

Standing in front of Akhkharu was Sebastian, they were squared off. Sebastian covered in blood splatter, smacking his club onto his left hand, Akhkharu hunched over with his massive arms extended and claws out ready to pounce. Fred had taken a step back so he wasn't standing directly in the way. To test if his powers were truly gone during the eclipse Sebastian grabs one of the stereos that was left behind by the flash mob and launches it at his foe.

Appearing weakened by the eclipse Akhkharu tries to block the stereo with his ability , but fails and it crashes into his chest. Seeing this Sebastian sprints forward raring back with his mace to swing when he is close enough. Akhkharu reels slightly from impact and rushes into a defensive position in anticipation of our own big man's attack.

The crack of bone on bone fills the air as Sebastian makes contact with the bull-like left leg of Akhkharu. Buckling at the knee Akhkharu went down. As he fell he took multiple swipes with his clawed hands, only one connected. I could see Sebastian drop his arm, covering his side. A small trail of blood leaked out from under his arm. This gave a chance to get back to his feet and lunge at him. Sebastian blocked the claws with his club batting them away with his powerful swings.

With a mighty downward swing with both of Akhkharu's hands, Sebastian hold his club above his head to block. The driving force pushed Sebastian to a knee. Holding with every ounce of strength Sebastian stayed firm in his placement. The great claws looked like they were cutting into the bone mace, digging deeper as he pushed down.

I see Fred running towards the battling behemoths with what looks like a giant cleaver. Pulling off my jacket to free the shotgun I rush in. Fred does a diving swing with the cleaver connecting to the back of Akhkharu's right knee. The god lets out an agonizing roar. As his balance starts to go Akhkharu grabs Fred by the ankle as he is trying to roll away and launches him through the air sending him crashing into a parked car on the street.

My window was open for an attack so I fire off three rounds as quickly as I could aim. The first hitting Akhkharu in the left shoulder weakening his attack on Sebastian. The second found its home in the thigh right above the gash Fred made. The third and final blew out the back of the left knee. Not having time to waste I jumped as high as I could, grabbing the shotgun with both hands. I felt the charge in my body build and dim blue glow intensified to a blinding electric light.

I swing the ax blade down as hard as I can muster. The razor edge splits the skull on impact and is buried down to the spine. I can feel a faint struggle caused by the nerves of Akhkharu through the grip of the weapon and yell "GET DOWN!!!" Hoping Sebastian heard me I pull the trigger sending the creatures face flying in all directions from the blast.

The beast's body goes limp and collapses to the ground. I see Sebastian wiping what I think is brain matter from his face with his shirt sleeve and I say "Dude, I'm so sorry. Did you not hear me yell to get down?"

Spitting out some of what got in his mouth and cleaning of his face a little more Sebastian stopped and gave me a disgusted glare and says "I was a little busy. It still had some fight in it."

Flicking some of the beast goo off of my shotgun I see Jenny, Mother and Jacqueline come out from the front of the building. Jenny runs straight for me and I run over to meet her halfway. Scooping her up in my arms I hug her tight. Setting her down I say "Did you see that shit?"

She took my face in her hands and looks my dead in the eyes and says "A fucking flash mob, that was your brilliant plan."

Smiling I say "Hey, it worked didn't it?"

She backs up a step and puts a finger in my face saying "You got lucky this time. Don't try that shit again before checking, got it?" I shake my head yes and she says "Good, now kiss me you idiot." We kiss and I can feel her spark on my lips.

When we were done I see Mother tending to Sebastian's side where Akhkharu claw had got him, Jacqueline is seeing to Fred who was sticking half out of a car window. Mother waves me over and Jenny and I jog over to see what she needs. Upon getting there Mother says "You need to finish this." pointing at the corpse of Akhkharu. "If his body remains whole, there's a chance he can come back."

Looking at the bloody mess in front of us I say "I'm not even sure where to start. Do I just cut it into pieces or what?"

Sebastian stands next to me looking over his club and says "I got dibs on the femur. This one is ruined." Picking up the cleaver that Fred had dropped, Sebastian starts hacking on the joint until it comes free.

Following his lead I take the ax and begin separating the arm from the shoulder. As each limb is removed we toss them into piles. Severing elbows, knees the remaining bit of its head leaving only the torso. The torso was still too big to manage by one of us and needs to be broken into smaller chunks. As I chop, I become more and more coated in the gods blood. The blood seemed to be absorb into my blackened skin giving me a boost of energy.

Splitting the ribs on the front and flip the torso over I whacked straight down the spine giving us two halves to haul away. With the final swing of the ax the house behind us let out a groan and the mist dissipated leaving no trace it was ever there.

The others had already begun hauling the body parts away. I slip the sling back over my shoulder and look down at the piles of mangles parts deciding to attempt to carry half of the torso over to Jacqueline's car. Hoisting it onto my shoulder I fling blood and organs to the ground. I walk to the car dragging a trail of intestines no longer caring if I make a mess.

Jacqueline had ran up to my apartment and grabbed trash bags so we wouldn't destroy the inside of her car with our carnage. Piece by piece go into its own bag, tying them off and tossing them in the trunk. Sebastian claims his prize limb setting it to the side, I start to bag the monster lower arm and decide to get a little trophy for myself. Borrowing Sebastian's knife I cut off two of the dragon talons and cram them in my cargo pocket. I bag the rest of the limb into the bag and put it with the rest.

Once her car was loaded down with body parts, I toss the keys to the work truck to Sebastian so him and Mother could follow Jacqueline and Fred. Jenny and I head to her car so we can convoy to the planned dumping grounds that we picked out. Doing maintenance from time to time you have to find new out of the way places to dispose of stuff the trash people won't take in the dumpster.

Firing up the Camaro the CD player kicks on playing Body Farm by Butcher making me laugh. Jenny reaches to turn it and I stop her saying "Leave it, it's appropriate." I start driving with the others following close behind.

We make several stops only dropping one of the bags at each location. A construction site here and there. Burying a few in freshly poured concrete as far as we could push it down. Other chunks made their way into the roadway under the newly repaired sink holes. The two halves of the torso were take to Jacqueline's store and into the furnace one at a time, making sure to clean the ashes out each time and bagging them separately.

Jacqueline dumped the contents from one of bags of ashes into a glass jar and mixed in a few of her mysterious herbs and sealed the jar with wax. She places a charm around the jar to finish it off with a little extra mojo. Jacqueline repeated this process with the other bag of ashes. Both were taken one at a time and placed in the hidden room.

We all left in teams of two once the last part was hidden away. Mother and Sebastian said their goodbyes and told us they would be in touch as soon as Sebastian healed up. Fred agrees to stay with Jacqueline for a few days or at least until he knew she would be safe and maybe do a little bit of remodeling to the front of the store. It was awfully generous considering it was him and his old buddies that messed it up. As for Jenny and I we chose to go back to her place for a while for a few reasons. My street is probably swarmed with cops looking for a monster war. Another reason is I have no lock or door handle on the door to my apartment, and finally my bed is soaked in blood.

Jenny drives her car and I follow behind in my work truck. We were going to stop for food but I convince her that we can get delivery since I'm still glowing a tiny bit and I'm drenched in blood from head to toe. After I park in front of her place she stops me outside to say she has roommates but she doesn't see their cars so we should just hurry in getting cleaned up.

I waste no time getting into the shower while she checked out the rest of the house to see if we were alone. Getting out of the shower I see a stack of clean clothes waiting for me. Getting dressed I walk out of the bathroom and see her gathering something to change into after she showers and I say "Thanks for the clothes, but should I be concerned why you have extra men's clothes here."

She bumps me with her shoulder as she walks passed me and says "Dick, they belong to Sarah's boyfriend. He won't even notice they're gone." Closing the door behind her I hear her say "I order food so get the door if they show up before I'm out."

Before I can reply to her I hear a bang on the front door. I make my way down stairs and open the door. I find a note nailed up to the door by four daggers. Ripping the daggers out of the door I take the note and read it to myself.

I close the door and head back to Jenny's room with note and daggers in hand. Jenny finishes her shower to find me sitting on her bed and says "Was that the food already, that was fast."

Handing her the note I say "not exactly, read this."

Jenny takes it and reads aloud "We know who you are Demigod and you have something that belongs to us. Signed the knights twelve."

To be continued…..

Watch for Visions of Knight